Montgomery House

By Katharine E. Hamilton

ISBN- 10: 0-692-91409-9
ISBN-13: 978-0-692-91409-0

Montgomery House

www.katharinehamilton.com

Cover Design by Kerry Prater.

To my Daddy.
A man of many talents, strong work ethic,
and a kind heart.

Acknowledgments

Thanks to my husband, Brad, for supporting me and loving my quirky self.

And thanks again to my Daddy for his knowledge on this one. Any mistakes are on my end.

Thanks to my alpha and beta reader team. I can always count on honest feedback and fun conversations when working with a manuscript.

Thanks to my editor, Lauren Hanson. I love that you will always know my struggles with 'past' and 'passed.' Ha!

And thanks to my readers. You guys are amazing. I appreciate you more than you know.

« CHAPTER ONE »

Liz Montgomery awoke to the sound of violent winds blowing and breaking against the sides of the old house. Glancing at the bedside clock, she noticed the time blinking. *Great,* she thought. *The electricity had flickered off in last night's storm.* She rose up and grabbed her cell phone and looked at the time. 7:45 AM. Sliding out of bed, she stretched as she shuffled towards the bathroom across the hall, and sleepily fumbled with the knobs to the shower. Steam began to fill the room and Liz slipped inside the opaque stall to let the hot water awaken her tired muscles.

Fifteen minutes later, and feeling like a new woman, she sat in the kitchen sipping her first cup of coffee on a wooden stool smoothly curved from years of use. She gazed over her schedule for the day. Her feminine, floral daily planner turned open and spread out on the bar as she absentmindedly stirred her coffee. The contractor was scheduled to come at 9:00 AM to survey the house and the porch. “No telling how long that will take,” she mumbled under her breath.

Liz’s grandparents’ old plantation style home stood outside the small town of Quinton, Georgia. The town, a beacon of Southern charm—and some arrogance— she admitted, was the embodiment of grace and fortitude. The town boasted of long standing traditions dating back to the Civil War, though Liz often found that said traditions were made up on the fly by some of the townspeople. Whatever suited them best in the moment seemed to be the word of the day. But overall, the cascading waves of wisteria and crepe myrtles coloring the sidewalks and offering a brief respite from the hot, Georgia sun, gave the historic old town a resolute beauty that never aged, but instead captured a slice of small town America in quaint streets and friendly faces.

Liz grew up in Quinton, born and then raised by her grandparents after her seventh birthday. The loss of her parents, though painful, just resided as an ache now. Her memories of her father and mother were vague, at best, so other than the feeling of loss, the sting of their untimely death had long since passed. Her grandparents were her parents. They loved her. Looked after her. Raised her. And she felt, though she may have been a bit biased, that they had done a stand-up job. The old house creaked as a strong gust of wind swished outside. The familiar sounds of tired stairs and frail doorframes filled the room as creaks and groans settled.

Liz loved growing up in Quinton, but after high school graduation the city called her name, not in a subtle whisper, but in a shout. She wanted out of the small town life. She wanted skyscrapers, jet planes, people, enormous amounts of people—and that is what Atlanta offered. She graduated from Georgia State University with a degree in Business and set out to make her mark. After owning several small businesses in the city, Liz did indeed make her mark. She found her niche in retail boutiques, and after starting up her own chain, she knew she wanted to extend her brand to Quinton's beautiful downtown and tap into the tourist market the town acquired each spring and fall. Her grandmother, Sissy Montgomery, owned a small retail space downtown, and like many other older buildings in town, it sat empty. Liz's decision to move back to Quinton was in part due to her grandfather's failing health and the opportunity to open a boutique in her grandmother's building was a large draw. And though she had finally wrapped up her life in the city last year, she was only able to spend a grand total of two weeks with her grandfather before he passed on. He now rested in the family cemetery secluded at the back of the family property. Montgomerys as far back as 1809 had graced the hills of Quinton, and what was once a sprawling, active plantation now only contained the large home surrounded by a couple hundred acres of lush pastureland that Liz's grandfather leased out to local cattle farmers, a business arrangement Liz hoped to continue for the future so as to make the most of the land. The extra income didn't hurt, either. Liz and her grandmother now resided together, though in separate wings of the house, and the aging residence needed some tender loving care that Liz hoped to provide.

Life would be different back in Quinton, she knew, but thus far, she found herself excited about the opportunity to refresh her family home while also starting a new business. A contented sigh slipped through her lips as she looked over her checklist for the day once again. The movers should arrive around noon with her belongings from Atlanta. She realized then that she would need some help with that, so she phoned her best friend since childhood, Anna.

Still stuck to her teacher schedule, Liz knew Anna would already be awake pacing her house with coffee-infused energy and looking for a way to start her summer break.

"Hello?" Anna answered.

"Well, you sound chipper," Liz replied.

Anna laughed. "Well, maybe I am having a good morning. You sound like you are still on your first cup of coffee."

Liz smiled. Anna knew her too well sometimes. "That I am. Hey, I was wondering if you could help me out today? The movers are coming, and well, I'm guessing I should get started on making this house presentable and livable."

"Woo Hoo!" exclaimed Anna. "Liz Montgomery living in Quinton! Thought I would never see you here again! Yes, I will be there. I'm about done with breakfast, and I was going to run up to the hardware store and drop off some breakfast for Ben and then I will head over. Unless you want to ride with me to the store?" Anna invited nonchalantly, her voice laced with a subtle hint of mischief.

Liz knew Anna's boyfriend, Ben Wheeler, star quarterback of the 2004 Quinton Football State Championship team— because such titles were remembered, honored, and appreciated in Quinton— would definitely appreciate a hot breakfast and the opportunity to see Anna. "Actually, a pit stop to the hardware store is on my list for today, so I would not mind at all."

"Great! I'll be over there in five," Anna responded and hung up without further discussion.

Liz hopped off her barstool and rushed back upstairs to her bedroom to dress, knowing full well Anna would be right on time. On her way up, she narrowly missed bumping into her grandmother. "My goodness!" Sissy clasped a hand over her heart as she leaned against the stair banister. "What on Earth has you in such a rush this mornin', Lizzy?"

"Sorry, Grandmother. I am heading into town with Anna to grab a few things at the hardware store before my meeting with the contractor." Liz nudged an unruly wave of hair out of her eyes as she continued up the steps. "She will be here soon. Have to hurry!" she called over her shoulder with an absent wave. Liz quickly dabbed some make up on her face and stepped out on the front porch just in time to see Anna pull up to the house.

"Perfect timing," Liz answered, as she crawled into Anna's vibrant blue Volkswagen beetle.

"What is that smell that is *so* divine?" Liz asked, twisting in her seat to look behind her.

Anna grinned. "I stopped and picked up donuts for the store." She motioned towards her backseat where four large boxes of donuts sat. Liz looked back to her friend. "Whoa, Ben needs that much?"

Anna rolled her eyes. "No, crazy. He asked if I could bring some for the other guys today, because they apparently have a lot of training sessions and meetings happening today."

Liz reached back into the seat and opened a box. She grabbed a donut and then sat back in her seat.

"Lizzy!" Anna scolded.

"What? It's just one," Liz replied, her mouth full of warm melting sugar.

The women pulled up to the hardware store and hopped out each carrying two bright pink boxes of donuts.

Liz followed Anna inside, her nerves on edge as she noted all the different handsaws to her left. Why there were so many different kinds when surely one could do just about any job, she didn't know. Her eyes traveled up the row to hammers. *Same here,* she thought, a bit overwhelmed. Men and women walked around the busy store as they made their way to the employees' area behind a work counter and what looked to be a warehouse space in the back. She noted multiple machines running as men loaded and unloaded lumber into the backs of waiting trucks. Anna waved at several people as she made her way towards the counter. Liz felt like a fish in a shark tank at the zoo as several people openly stared at her as she walked by with Anna. Yes, she knew she had been gone from Quinton a long time, but the smell of fresh meat had every employee and customer gawking as they passed.

∞

Jackson Dean hung up the phone in his office and barked at his assistant. No one replied. He stood, annoyed that the young woman held little interest in her work and more interest in the various men around the shop or Solitaire on her computer. He walked towards the main counter, "Rebecca!" he belted. "I've called you several times, why are you not at your desk?!" His firm demand carried forth throughout the room. He froze as he rounded the corner and saw Rebecca, along with everyone else, had left her work and desk to surround two women with donuts.

Anna Richards, Ben's girlfriend, and one of her friends— *a very beautiful friend*— stood with open boxes of donuts for men and women to grab by the handfuls.

He noticed several men trying to strike conversation with the friend, but she seemed impervious to their efforts. She simply smiled politely and kept offering them the round delicacies of sugar.

He watched her a minute. Her long, chestnut hair was pulled back into a sleek, high ponytail that made her face look thin and delicate. Her dark eyes smiled as she laughed at some of the comments the workmen made. She was not a short woman, but neither was she very tall. Jackson realized then that he considerably liked her appearance and height.

"Rebecca!" he barked again, causing several of the workmen to flinch. Liz noticed several nervous glances as they all quickly grabbed donuts and departed. Rebecca darted towards the tall man on the other side of the room.

"Yes sir, Mr. Dean. What can I do to help you, sir?" Rebecca asked nervously. Jackson eyed the donuts in her hands and she slowly pulled them behind her back as though she had been caught red-handed in the cookie jar.

Jackson handed her a file. "This is the Reagan bid. I need you to fax it to the number on the cover page. Then, you need to call and verify they received it. After that, I would like an email confirming the bid's delivery."

"Yes sir," Rebecca answered and quickly darted to her desk and began typing on her keyboard.

"My goodness," a sweet, Southern drawl filtered through the air and had him turning back towards Ben's girlfriend, only her friend walked towards him. "Sounds like someone could use a donut this mornin'." She grinned as she opened the box towards him.

"I'm fine, thank you." He dismissed her with a nod as he turned back towards his office. To his retreating back he heard a muffled "Scrooge," as she turned back towards Ben and Anna.

"A Scrooge, am I?" He noted the surprise in her eyes as she spun around and noticed he stood in the doorway watching her.

She flapped the lid open and closed so the sweet aroma filtered through the air. "Who turns down donuts from a beautiful woman?" Ben called to him with a grin.

"Fine." He sighed. "I'll take one."

"No." She flapped the lid closed as he reached for one.

"What? Why?" he asked in surprise.

"Listen… sir," she paused as she realized she had no idea what his name was.

"Jackson." He supplied his name.

"Jackson," she replied. His name had never sounded sweeter, he realized, and he liked the sass with which she delivered it. "These are donuts," she began again as she opened the lid. "Donuts are not something you have to be talked into. They are what you gorge yourself on and then feel upset with yourself afterwards for eating too many. They are a happy food. One which you should jump at the chance of eating. They make people happy. You are not happy. Therefore, you do not get a happy food." She gave him a challenging expression as she snapped the box closed.

He sighed and shrugged his shoulders. "I see. Well, I guess I will just go back to my office. Unhappy, alone, no donut." He turned his body as if he were about to walk away but quickly turned back around and snatched the box out of her hands. She gasped in shock and quickly lunged for the box.

Jackson turned and blocked her from taking it back. He tossed another donut to a smiling Ben. He then snatched a donut and took a bite. He held it in his mouth as he closed the lid. He handed her the box back, and removed the donut from his mouth and flashed a wide grin.

"Thanks for the donut." He tapped her nose to irritate her, and then turned to walk towards his office.

She turned and saw Ben and Anna smiling at her frustrated stance.

She huffed and motioned over her shoulder. "Who is that man?"

"Jackson Dean." Her friends walked towards her as Ben motioned towards the back offices. "He's a new contractor we brought on board a few weeks ago."

"Dean?" Liz asked, her brows rising. "As in the Willow Lane Deans?"

Ben nodded. "One and the same."

"You hired a Dean?"

Ben held up his hands in a calming gesture. "Take it easy, Liz. He's a good guy."

"I didn't say anything," she defended, casting a curious glance towards the man's office door. "I just didn't realize there were more of them."

Anna grinned. “Any cute ones, you mean?”

Liz rolled her eyes. “No, Anna.” She walked towards the aisle containing the array of hammers she passed by earlier and began browsing. “I’m just surprised my grandmother didn’t mention any new Deans. We all know that would be a hot topic.”

“I imagine she doesn’t know.” Ben shrugged as he walked forward and pulled a hammer off the rack and handed it to her. “Pretty universal one,” he commented, as she slipped it into a basket.

“My grandmother would know if there was another Dean breathing the same air as she was.” Liz moved towards nails and looked to Ben blankly. “Seriously, why does there need to be so many choices?”

Laughing, Ben crossed his arms. “What are you needing to put together, Liz?”

She shrugged. “I don’t know, an old house. Not sure if you’ve noticed, but my grandparents’ house is sort of caving in on itself.”

“And you think a hammer and nails will fix it?”

“It’s a start,” she grumbled as she pulled a nail from the drawer in front of her and surveyed its length before putting it back. “I’m meeting with a contractor at nine.”

"A contractor?" Ben asked with a bit of confusion. "I didn't realize you were on our list."

"Oh it's not one of your guys," she answered. "Grandmother wanted me to find one from Atlanta. No offense." She grimaced as she looked up at him. "Though if it makes you feel any better, we've already had three refuse to take on the project of remodeling the house."

"Why?"

"Why, Ben Wheeler," Anna walked up and ran her hand over his shoulder as she grinned at Liz. "Don't you know the Montgomery Plantation is haunted?"

Liz shook her head. "Apparently."

"Haunted? Since when?" Ben looked to Anna.

"Since Liz's grandfather died." Her voice quieted out of respect as she gauged Liz's reaction.

"It's true." Liz confirmed. She looked up as Ben's skepticism flashed across his face. "Okay, wait," she waved her hand. "I'm not confirming that my house is haunted, I'm just confirming that that is the current belief. Apparently there have been 'sightings' of my grandfather's ghost in the house and on the property."

"Scaring away any potential contractors," Anna finished for her.

Liz waved her hand to acknowledge the validity of Anna's statement.

"That is ridiculous." Ben shook his head as he grabbed Liz's basket and walked it towards the counter. "If you had come to me, I could have hooked you up with a great contractor." He pointed towards Jackson Dean's office door.

"A Dean?" Liz stood baffled. "There is no way Sissy Montgomery is going to have a Dean working on her family home."

"Isn't that family rivalry a bit old by now?" Ben asked. "Besides, Jackson isn't anything like his family. He just moved here and doesn't have anything to do with the old feud."

"And you think my grandmother will care? Clearly you have lost your mind. The day a Dean steps foot on Montgomery property will be the next Civil War. No matter what I think, you think, or Jackson Dean thinks." Liz reached into her purse and grabbed her wallet. Pointing to her full basket she asked, "So, what's the damage?"

«CHAPTER TWO»

Jackson sat in his chair and sifted through another bid. It was a small project that would allow him to grocery shop for the week, but not help him kick start his business. He ran a hand through his hair; the dark mass needed a cut, but the task ranked low on his priorities at the moment. If business did not pick up soon, he would find himself in a major deficit. His office door swung open and a smiling Ben Wheeler stood in his doorway. He clapped his hands once before sliding into the chair across from Jackson's desk. "You can thank me ahead of time." He waved his hand towards Jackson.

Confused, Jackson's forehead wrinkled. "Thank you?"

"You're welcome." Ben grinned. "I believe I just found you your next client."

"Oh really? And who might that be?"

"My friend Liz who was just here."

"The woman with the donuts?"

"One and the same."

"And what is she needing done?"

"She just moved back from Atlanta to her old family home and is looking to remodel and refurbish it. She needs a contractor. You head over there at nine."

"Nine? Today?" he asked, glancing at his watch. "That's in thirty minutes."

"Then I guess you better get a move on." Ben handed him a slip of paper with an address on it. "Now, I got you the interview and the look-see, but you have to win the bid."

"Easy enough." Jackson extended his hand. "Thanks man. I appreciate this."

"Don't mention it. Let me know how it goes."

Jackson gathered his car keys and a notepad from his desk and hurried out to his truck.

As he made his way through Quinton and turned down the long winding road that led just outside downtown, he spotted the heavy clouds rolling in that promised the chance of a summer storm. He rolled up his windows on the off chance the clouds decided to relinquish their liquid contents. He spotted the arched entryway, a brick wall with black ironwork scrolls traipsing across the top and the whimsical letter 'M' in the center. *Fancy place*, he thought, as he pulled to the gate and pressed the intercom button.

"May we help you?" A voice, deep in Georgia roots and edged with a soft rasp slid through the speaker.

"Contractor from Wheeler's Hardware. Have an appointment at nine." He waited a moment before a buzz filtered through and the large, wrought iron gate slowly began to open.

The driveway was lined with stately oaks, the overlapping limbs and leaves creating a canopied tunnel leading up to a massive, white pillared house. He pulled to a stop in the circle drive behind another vehicle and slid out of his truck. Ben failed to mention that his friend Liz was rich— *not that it mattered*, he told himself, but he despised feeling intimidated, and yet there he was, intimidated by an old, crumbling house. He walked up the front steps, the uneven terrain not going unnoticed, nor the rotting beams above his head. Yes, the house needed work, but the timeless beauty still remained. He grabbed the brass knocker and released two loud raps on the door.

Waiting only a moment, it opened and a portly woman in her early sixties, he guessed, looked him up and down.

"You're the contractor?" the same raspy voice from the intercom asked him.

"Yes ma'am."

"We already have a contractor here. I didn't realize Ms. Lizbeth double booked. Come in." She stepped back and allowed him to enter the main entry. His breath caught at the worn beauty of the place. *Oh how he would love to get his hands on this,* he thought, as she led him to a sitting parlor.

"I do not know when she will be done with the other contractor, but I will let her know you are here. Would you like some tea?"

"Tea would be nice, thank you."

She nodded as she stepped out of the room.

He took the time to study the mantle work above the fireplace. The marble was smooth and cool to the touch, the workmanship remarkable. *What it must be like to live in a home so full of history,* he wondered. He heard voices coming from the entryway before Liz and a robust man with sunburned skin stepped into the parlor. Her eyes widened in surprise. "Jackson," she eyed him curiously. "I didn't realize you were here." She turned to the other man and offered a polite smile, a smile he did not return as he eyed Jackson.

"I did not realize you had another contractor lined up," the man asked.

"I don't," Liz assured him. "Do you know each other?" she asked.

Jackson shook his head, but the man nodded. "Seems a few of my potential clients put me on the backburner to use you instead." His disgruntled attitude made Jackson's shoulders stiffen.

"I have not intended to steal clients, mister—" He extended his hand to the man in order to catch his name, but the man scoffed.

"Stealin' is what you gone and done, sonny. There's no room for more contractors in this town. It's hard enough competin' with the hardware store. Don't need you to add to it."

"I am sorry you feel that way. But as I hear it, Ms. Liz here has had a hard time finding a contractor due to the mysterious happenings here."

Liz's face paled slightly as the man turned to her. "What mysterious happenings?"

"It's nothing, really," she tried to keep her tone light as she eyed Jackson with scolding blue eyes. "You know how people can be when it comes to old houses. Ghosts, hauntings, superstitions. It seems my grandparents' home is just the recent target of such rumors."

"Hauntings?" the man asked. "I don't mess with no haunted houses, miss. That voodoo stuff is serious." He took his hat in his hand and placed it on his head. "You win this one." He looked to Jackson. "I ain't got time to be cursed." And with that, he stormed out of the house as if he'd been bitten.

"Gee, thanks," Liz commented dryly as she motioned for him to sit. "Other than running off my potential contractor, why are you here?"

Jackson looked confused. "You asked me to be."

"I'm sorry?" she asked. "I did not ask you to come to my house."

"Ben said you needed a contractor and that you wanted to meet with me at nine."

"He lied." Liz folded her hands in her lap, the gesture spoke of years of etiquette classes as he watched her cross her feet at the ankles and sit straight in her chair.

"I see." Jackson felt embarrassed, as he gathered his notepad and brought it to his lap to stand. "Well then I guess I will head on out then. I did not realize he was inviting me to offer a bid that was not asked for. I apologize for the inconvenience."

Standing, he offered a polite nod before turning towards the exit.

"Now wait a minute," she called out after him. He turned, the look of uncertainty on his face had her shoulders relaxing.

"Obviously I still need a contractor," she waved her hand towards the sound of a departing vehicle. "One who is not afraid of ghosts, or the potential appearance of ghosts. Do you qualify?"

"I think I could handle a few ghosts, if need be." He walked back towards his seat and sat.

Liz studied him closely. "How come I've never heard of you?"

"What do you mean?" he asked.

"You're a Dean. I know all of the Deans in Quinton."

"Ah," he scratched the stubble at his chin before answering. "Well I just recently moved back."

"So Ben said. From where?"

"Michigan."

"Michigan? You're a Yankee?"

The southern distaste in her tone made him smirk as he leaned forward. "I was born in Georgia, if that makes it better."

"It doesn't. You left. How in the world do you think you can start a business in Quinton if you're a Yankee? Don't you know that people here still hold a grudge?"

"I'm starting to see that." He pointed his pencil at her as he leaned back in his chair and rested his arm on the armrests.

"I don't hold a grudge, I'm just pointing out that some people will," Liz clarified.

"I see. So is this you saying you will give me a chance to come up with a bid?"

"No." She saw his shoulders slightly slump in disappointment before he recovered with a forced smile.

"I see."

"I will not deny you a bid based on whether or not you are a Yankee. Your reasons for moving above the Mason-Dixon are your own. My decision to pass you up is based on the fact that you are a Dean."

"A Dean? What is wrong with my family?"

She sighed heavily as if he were a simpleton and that her time was more valuable than being spent explaining. "Don't you know?"

"Know what?" He tossed his hands up with impatience.

"The Montgomerys and the Deans despise one another."

"Why?"

"Seriously?!" she asked, her eyes round. "You don't know?"

"Obviously not. Enlighten me, oh sweet Ms. Montgomery," he retorted, his mockery not going unnoted.

"Our families have hated one another since the Civil War. Literally," she stated. "Something about your great, great, great, great... well, I don't know how many greats, but your Granddaddy hated my granddaddy, so-and-so was a southern sympathizer, and you –know-who sided with the north. Bang-bang, so-and-so was shot and killed, and family blood was spilt." She waved her hand as if the story were old news and details unimportant.

"So because my great, great, great... however many greats, Granddaddy hated your however many greats Granddaddy, you can't hire me to fix your house?" He shook his head and sneered. "This is the most ridiculous thing I have ever heard." He shuffled as if about to stand and leave.

"Me too." she agreed, bringing his attention back to her face.

"Then why won't you give me a chance?"

"Because it is not just me who lives here. My grandmother, Sissy Montgomery, holds strong objections against the Dean family. The Civil War started a family rivalry, but generation after generation has fueled the fire, so to speak. She'd probably die before letting a Dean touch her home."

"With all due respect to your grandmother, I find this all totally insane." Jackson tucked his pen behind his ear. "I don't even know her and she doesn't even know me, so how could she hate me? Seems a bit immature."

Liz shrugged. "It's just how things stand."

"So you're still not going to give me a shot?"

"I'll have to think on it. She'll question your education and training as well. There's much to consider."

"Well you can ease her fears. I was born in Georgia, raised in Michigan, college in California, and now I'm back here."

"And that is supposed to help?" Liz asked with a slight tilt to the lips. "A Yankee and a hippie? You're just hurting your cause."

He was close to storming out until he saw the light twinkle in her eye at the word 'hippie.'

"Well can this 'hippie' at least take a look around to get an idea of what you need or want done to the place?"

She eyed him a moment, her steely eyes sharp as she nodded. "Sure. I'll show you around. Who knows, after you see the poor shape of the place you may be the one rejecting me." Standing, she waved for him to follow. "We can start outside. I'm sure you noticed the shape of the porch when you arrived."

"I did, yes."

She opened the front door and stepped onto the creaking porch.

"So are you looking to repair anything and everything that needs it?" Jackson asked, already making notes on his pad as he walked around the porch checking railings, pillars, and boards.

"Yes. And on the inside of the house I not only want to repair, but also update and remodel some areas. Mainly the kitchen," Liz explained, watching him closely as he got onto his hands and knees and peered underneath the porch. *More of a survey than the last guy,* she thought.

"This could take a while." Jackson stood and brushed his knees off. "For a thorough bid, I'm going to need to look this place over with a fine tooth comb."

"Be my guest. My grandmother isn't here, so if you want to look it over top to bottom, now is the time. I can show you her wing of the house first so that she will not interrupt us."

"Sounds good." He followed her back inside and she led the way up the sweeping staircase and turned right. "So should I receive your grandmother's approval, I can pretty much start right away. Most of my crew's projects are wrapping up right now, so it shouldn't take us long to get started. Again... if she approves."

"My grandmother trusts my judgment," Liz stated as she flicked the light switch to a large ballroom that was now used as a formal sitting and dining room. "But should I decide to use you as our contractor, we will keep your last name under wraps."

He shook his head in disbelief and she paused to look him in the eye. "I'm serious, Jackson. When you are in this house your last name will not be spoken. My grandmother has her own reasons for not liking your family, and they run deep. I don't want to upset her."

"But I hardly have anything to do with that. I know nothing." Defending himself, he stretched his arms as if to present himself as he was.

"I know. I haven't done anything either, and yet, I imagine your family would dislike me as well."

"Look, my grandmother, Ginger Dean, has never said anything to me about the Montgomerys."

"Your grandmother is Ginger? Which son do you belong to?"

"David Dean."

Liz squinted. "Never heard of him." She crossed her arms as she waited for him to continue.

"Because when he moved away from Georgia, his ties with the family were severed. I've just started regaining my grandmother's affections. The fact that I am, as you say, a Yankee and a hippie, does not sit well with my family either. Unfortunately."

"So why come back to Quinton?"

"It's a beautiful place. I have family here that I never got to know and want to. A history. I didn't quite have the easiest childhood in Michigan. When my grandmother heard I was looking for a new place to plant roots, she invited me to live in Quinton."

"That's sweet of her," Liz acknowledged, as she watched him make notes on his pad and then run his palm over a baseboard on the north wall. He scribbled some more.

"She's a sweet lady," he added. "Course, I'm sure you wouldn't know about that considering you are probably forbidden to speak to her."

"I've spoken to Ginger Dean multiple times. She is a nice lady. I never said otherwise. Just because my grandmother has a problem with her doesn't mean I do. I moved away from Quinton as well, remember."

"And why did you?" Jackson looked up and she realized then how dark his eyes were. A deep brown, almost black, that would make his face seem hard were it not for the easy way he smiled. His dark hair framed a firm face of angles and a jaw boasting a small cleft in his chin. *He made an appealing picture*, she thought. She realized she was staring and blinked before turning towards one of the windows. "This window has a crack." She pointed and he tapped his notepad.

"Yeah, I've got that written down."

"Oh." She wound her hands together in front of her as they stood studying one another. Voices drifted up the stairs and her eyes widened. Gasping softly, she rushed towards him and pulled him towards the far side of the room. "That's my grandmother. She can't see you."

"I thought if we kept my last name quiet, we would be fine." Jackson silenced as her hand flew over his mouth and her eyes were sharp.

"Shhhh," she whispered. "Follow me." She pulled him by the hand towards a bookshelf beside the fireplace, pulled a book, and the shelf eased away from the wall. She opened it and slid inside, dragging him behind her. She quickly pulled the faux door closed behind them. Jackson's eyes widened as he surveyed the narrow hallway.

She looked up at him in the small space and a sly grin spread over her face. "Did I mention we have secret passages?" Her whisper was quiet as they heard Sissy Montgomery ordering their maid to bring her tea. "Follow me," Liz whispered, and began leading the way down the hall to their left.

∞

A series of turns and twists had Jackson losing his sense of direction in the house, but Liz seemed intent on her destination. Before long, she came to a wall and pushed lightly against it. He heard the floor pull away and another door opened. She peeked into the awaiting room and then stepped out, waving him to follow. They entered another ballroom; the hard wood floors were marred with age but the only furnishing was a modern and comfortable couch, not at all like the previous ballroom. "This is my wing. Movers are bringing my belongings today." She explained. "My grandfather showed me all the secret passages in the house when I was a kid. Most of them were designed for former slaves. Though the Montgomerys fought for the south during the Civil War, they did not believe in the practice of slavery. Most slaves that were listed as servants for the Montgomerys were actually paid a small salary." Anyway," she motioned for him to sit on a long, cream sofa with more decorative pillows than he thought necessary, but he did appreciate the style they brought to the room. "The passages were used to hide slaves and household members during some of the invasions. Tended to work most of the time. Now the halls are just used as a means for me to get from one place or another in a quicker fashion."

"Or secretive fashion," he added, making her smile. "So you grew up here?"

"Yes. My parents passed when I was little. My grandparents raised me, and this is the house I grew up in."

"That must have been nice." He looked up at the elaborate ceiling and then to the decorative tapestries hanging on the walls. "I mean the house, not your parents passing. Sorry about that."

"It's alright. Sometimes it was great growing up here. Other times it was rather lonely." The focus he held on her face at that moment made her squirm and quickly change the subject. "So is this a type of project you think you could handle?"

He nodded. "I can handle pretty much anything."

"Confident." She smirked as he shrugged.

"I'm good at what I do."

"Okay, I'll rephrase the question," she continued. "Is this a project you would *want* to handle?"

His lips twitched into an easy smile. "Are you hiring me?"

She crossed her arms. "Potentially. Obviously I will need to see your final bid and ideas, but I need a contractor, as you pointed out earlier, and so far you don't seem freaked out about the prospect."

"I haven't seen any ghosts." He pointed at her as if she was holding out on him and she laughed.

"Well don't get your hopes up. I haven't either. But if you hear creepy whispers in the walls or better yet, the fireplaces—" his brow rose and she laughed. "Why, Mr. Dean, don't you know? We Montgomerys used to throw our servants in the fireplace if they disobeyed."

He looked surprised.

"A myth," she clarified. "But it seems we have the reputation of being heartless, and there stems the haunted nature of the house."

"That's a bit of a harsh rumor."

"It's how the rumor mill rolls in a small town. You'll get used to it."

"Well, I think I have a little of what I need. How about I create a bid just for what I've seen thus far and you see the extent of what I plan, and then if you like what you see I can come back and survey the rest of the house?"

She nodded and stood, brushing her hands over her jeans. "That sounds like a good plan. I appreciate you coming."

"Even though I sort of invited myself?" he asked on a laugh.

"You didn't. Ben invited you over, or tricked you to come over, I should say. He's just trying to help me out. That's another reason I'm willing to give you a shot. Ben wouldn't mislead me or recommend you unless he thought you would do a decent job."

"Even for a Dean?"

"Yet to be determined," she jested, as they made their way down the staircase.

"Lizbeth!" Her grandmother's voice drifted out of the parlor as she stepped into the entryway. Her sharp, hazel eyes roamed over Jackson before landing back on Liz. "I didn't realize you had company." The older woman, though tiny in stature, straightened her shoulders and stood regally awaiting introductions.

"Hello Grandmother," Liz began, "this is our potential new contractor. Ben sent him to look at the house." She smiled politely at Jackson as he stepped forward and extended his hand. Sissy

Montgomery stood with her hands clasped on the top of her cane, her gaze never wavering as she slowly lifted a hand to him. Her handshake was limp as he tried not to crush her delicate hand. "A pleasure to meet you, ma'am."

"You from Atlanta?" Her slow, southern drawl was edged with steel.

"No ma'am. I live here in Quinton."

"Who's your family?" her eyes squinted as they pored into him.

Liz stepped forward and lightly brushed their hands aside as she began nudging him towards the door. "Grandmother, not everyone has family here in Quinton. Sometimes people just want to live in a new place. Jackson here will be providing us with a bid to look at for the house sometime next week. Right, Jackson?" She turned to him and he nodded. "Yes ma'am. Next week." He was now on the front porch and Liz squeezed her way out the front door, closing it behind her. Her eyes widened as if they were sneaking out of the house on false pretenses. "Sorry about that. The longer we stayed in there the more questions she would ask."

"I understand." He tucked his pen behind his ear and extended his hand.

She reached out and took it, a slight warmth traced up Liz's arm and she tugged her hand back. "Thank you for coming, Mr. D—Jackson," she corrected. "Is it okay if I call you Jackson?"

"Sure."

Nodding, she pointed to herself. "Liz. Liz Montgomery."

"I gathered that." He smiled as she slightly flushed.

"Well we were never properly introduced, so I just wanted to—"

"Make sure you were on the up and up," he finished, drawing forth the nervous laugh he had hoped for.

"Yes. I guess you could say that."

"It's nice to meet you, Liz. I look forward to working with you."

"Potentially," she corrected.

"Potentially," he echoed with a slight nod of farewell. "Take care." He turned and traipsed back to his truck, while Liz stood on the front porch of the stately home watching him as he backed away.

He thought the house suited her, as he watched her in his rear view mirror until pulling through the sturdy entry gate. He paused a moment before turning onto the main drive and watched as she walked back into the house with a final wave, as if she knew he sat studying her.

«CHAPTER THREE»

"So what's the damage?" Anna asked, as she plopped her purse down on the bar and Liz turned from the fridge.

"Tea?" she asked her friend.

"Yes, please. It's so hot even Satan is sweatin' today." Anna dabbed a napkin to her forehead as Liz slid her a glass of sweet iced tea.

"It's only going to get hotter." Liz thumbed through Jackson's bid and turned to the last page, sliding it over to Anna.

Anna's eyes widened as she choked back on her sip. "Wow. That's… steep."

"And that's not all of it. That's just what he's seen. If you ask me, that's a generous bid."

"*How in the world*?" Anna placed a hand over her heart. "You think your grandmother is willing to part with her money?"

Liz laughed. "She's going to have to if this home is to withstand the next hundred years, or even the next year. I've run it by her, and she's impressed with his attention to detail, so it looks like I will be hiring him."

"And does she know he is a Dean?"

Liz shushed her and peeked through the kitchen doorway. "No, and neither does anyone else in this house."

"Wow. So you are going against family to hire him?"

"It's not going against family. The feud is ridiculous anyway, and it has nothing to do with us. He seems like a nice guy and—"

"And you like him," Anna pointed out.

Liz coughed and lightly patted her chest as she cleared her last sip of tea. "I did not say that. I said he was nice and was going to say, before I was so rudely interrupted, that he seems capable."

"Capable, right." Anna took a long swig of tea. "Capable," she repeated with a sly grin.

A snort escaped Liz as she started to laugh and she threw her napkin at Anna. "You are terrible." She grabbed a plate of tea cakes and walked towards the French doors off the kitchen. "Let's sit on the patio."

As they slid into their seats, Anna waved a hand towards the drive. "Looks like Ben is headed this way. He must be looking for me."

Both women waved as Ben pulled to a stop and hopped out of his truck. His face split into his charming smile as he walked up and accepted Anna's glass of tea. Gulping half of it down, he turned to Liz. "So you did it. You hired a Dean."

Liz waved him down. "Ben Wheeler, you will lose that pretty head of yours if you go around my house shoutin' Dean."

He cringed a bit as he looked towards the door. "Sorry, I didn't think she was here." He slid into a free seat.

"She is, but I think she is resting. And I do plan on hiring Jackson. I plan on telling him this afternoon."

"Good. He'll do a great job for ya, Liz."

"I believe he will. And no, my grandmother does not know he is a Dean."

"Do you really think she would care?" Anna asked.

Ben and Liz cast her appalled looks.

"This is Hatfield and McCoy stuff, Anna, of course she would care," Ben explained, patting her on the hand. "These type of family grudges don't just disappear. Besides, Liz's grandmother has her own reasons for hating the Dean family."

"But that was a long time ago. Plus, she found love with Liz's grandfather."

"But a woman scorned..." Liz trailed off. "She did love my grandfather, but her first love was Jackson's grandfather. The fact that he chose Ginger and broke my grandmother's heart has never been forgotten. Even my grandfather wished she would let go of her hurt, but she never really did. She's carried it with her through the years. If she knew Jackson was Ronald and Ginger Dean's grandson, she would fire him on the spot. And probably kill him for good measure." Liz tilted her glass towards Ben as he refilled Anna's and then hers.

"Does Jackson look anything like his grandfather? You think she will figure it out?" Anna asked.

"I have no idea. I've only seen Ronald Dean a handful of times, and I have no idea what he looked like as a younger man. She did eye Jackson pretty hard the other day, but she didn't mention anything to me."

"You think you can pull this off?" Ben asked, "Hiding his identity from her?"

"I will have to if she wants this house repaired." Liz's phone rang and she glanced at the caller id. "Speaking of," she held up her phone and her grandmother's name flashed on the screen.

"Hello Grandmother," she answered. "Yes, that is Ben Wheeler's truck you see in the drive. Yes, he and Anna are here visiting. Yes ma'am." Liz hung up. "Sometimes I feel like I'm in high school again. She's a bit of a spy."

Ben laughed. "Good luck hiding Jackson's name from her. That woman has eyes and ears everywhere. Obviously." He nodded to her phone.

Sighing, Liz leaned back in her chair. "Lord, help me."

Her friends laughed as they toasted towards her and her new quest of secrecy.

∞

Pulling into the drive of the Montgomery residence, Jackson checked his rearview mirror as several of his workmen pulled up behind him. Trailers of equipment and supplies began lining the driveway, and Liz stepped out onto the front porch holding her hand to shade her eyes as she watched. Jackson stepped out of his truck and walked up the steps.

"Well, well, well, Mr. Dean, looks like you've brought in the cavalry." Her voice was low as she turned to look in the open doorway. "Sorry, I mean, Jackson." She feigned a grimace as she stepped towards the steps to follow him down towards his truck.

"No time like the present to get started." He motioned towards his men as they began the work of unloading. "Hope your grandmother doesn't mind scaffolding on the exterior of her home for a few months."

"Her grandmother doesn't mind one bit."

They both turned at the sound of Sissy Montgomery's voice as she slowly made her way down the front steps, her cane less a statement of style than of necessity.

"Mrs. Montgomery," Jackson stepped forward and nodded a greeting. "Thank you for the opportunity to work on your beautiful home."

Sissy's eyes watched closely as Jackson's men began setting up on the east wing of the house. "It is my granddaughter who convinced me. I do not like to be disappointed."

Jackson, taken back by her sharpness, looked at Liz's apologetic face. "I only aim to please, ma'am."

"I do not like a lot of noise either. And if your men should enter the house, they are to be respectful of the antiques and my quiet as best they can."

"Grandmother," Liz tried to interrupt and her grandmother swiftly ended her interjection with a look.

"We will do our best to respect your home and your wishes, Mrs. Montgomery." Jackson offered as polite a smile as possible, but his hackles were still raised at the woman's attitude towards Liz.

"Lizbeth will be keeping me informed of your progress. Should I be disappointed in your work our contract is null and void." Without another word, Sissy turned and made her way back into the house.

"She's a charmer." Jackson commented and earned the fretful glance of Liz. "Sorry, that was uncalled for. I'm sure she's great."

"No, that's her usual sunny disposition," Liz admitted. "And she doesn't quite understand contracts."

He laughed. "Well, I will do my best not to disappoint her." Looking down at Liz, Jackson reached out and tucked a loose strand of her hair behind her ear. Realizing his actions, he cleared his throat and took a step back. "Guess we should get started. Excuse me." Awkwardly, he turned and walked away.

Liz watched him as he began barking orders at his workers and hopped into his truck to move it out of the way of another. "Lizbeth! Shut that door, girl, you're lettin' all the bought air out!" She cringed at her grandmother's harsh tone and stepped back into the house.

"Grandmother, you did not have to be rude to Jackson." Liz sat in the front parlor in a chair adjacent to Sissy's and reached for a glass of sweet tea.

"I was not rude." Her grandmother seemed surprised by the notion. "I was simply statin' my terms. I know nothin' about this boy, and I want to make sure he knows who is boss here."

"I believe you made that clear."

"Don't be sour, Lizbeth. It's uncomely."

Liz took a sip of her glass and set it back on the table. "I think I will make a trip to the grocery store. Anna and Ben plan to come by for supper tonight."

"In your wing, I hope. I prefer to eat alone in the dining hall," Sissy reminded her.

"Yes, Grandmother, in my wing. But I will need to use the kitchen down here to actually prepare the food. We will eat in the east wing."

"It will be nice once you have your own kitchen upstairs, won't it?"

"Yes, I think it will be. Jackson has drafted some beautiful plans for it."

"Good. I'm glad you're pleased." Sissy waved her hand. "On with ya now. Those groceries won't buy themselves."

Dismissed, Liz gathered her purse and headed out the door.

∞

Eyeing the list in her hand, Liz turned her shopping cart down aisle five and blew a frustrated breath as she saw the unlimited amount of choices when it came to pasta. She always wanted to be adventurous when it came to new foods, but her lack of prowess in the kitchen had her sticking rigidly to a recipe card. The difference between angel hair and regular spaghetti noodles, other than thickness, she didn't know. She also loved the look of bow tie pasta, but could not fathom using it in spaghetti. Could she?

"Elizabeth Montgomery?" A sweet voice dipped in Southern honey swam over Liz as she turned to find a smiling Ginger Dean walking towards her, basket in hand.

"Hello, Mrs. Dean." Liz awkwardly shifted the two boxes of pasta in her hands and placed them back on the shelf before she dropped them. Growing up she had hardly ever spoken with anyone in the Dean family for fear of her grandmother's reprimand, and here she was openly speaking to the matriarch in the grocery store and secretly conversing with the grandson on a daily basis. *What Sissy Montgomery would do to her hide if she found out.* She shuddered at the thought as she plastered a friendly smile on her face. "How are you?"

"I am doing just fine, dear." She patted her silver hair, freshly styled from what Liz assumed was her weekly beauty shop visit. "My Jackson has just been speakin' loads about you the last few days. Seems he's lovin' workin' on your house."

Liz's eyes widened and Ginger waved her hand. "Oh, don't worry dear, I know it's top secret." She covertly grabbed Liz's elbow and turned her away from the front of the store. "I just wanted to say thank you for givin' him a chance. He's had a hard go gettin' started here in Quinton, what with him bein' a foreigner and all."

"Foreigner?" Liz asked in confusion.

"You know," she leaned forward in a whisper. "Bein' a Yankee."

Liz couldn't help the smile that crept over her face as she nodded. "Ah, yes, of course, foreigner."

"But he really is a good boy, despite his daddy's problems. How Jackson turned out so well, we will never know. But so glad he has made friends with that Wheeler boy. They seem like two peas in a pod these days." She eyed Liz before stepping away. "From what I hear, you are mighty good friends with that Wheeler boy as well."

"Yes ma'am, I am. He dates my best friend Anna."

"Oh yes, sweet Anna. Well, I do hope Jackson is lucky enough to become friends with all of you. Why, with him workin' on your house I bet you will be seein' him every day for months. Somethin's bound to happen between the lot of ya."

"He seems like a very nice man, Mrs. Dean."

"Oh for certain. And handsome to boot." Ginger grinned. "Well, I've taken up enough of your time. I just wanted to say thank you again for lettin' Jackson take on your house. He says it really is quite extraordinary. Though I would not know, I've never stepped foot in it." She waved a hand in front of her face. "Woooo! Wouldn't Sissy Montgomery just have a fit if I walked into her house?!" She laughed, though Liz found the thought horrifying. "She'd call down all the spirits to evict me, I'm sure, and curse me straight to Hades." She shook her head and lightly patted Liz's arm. "I'm glad to see the next generation of Montgomerys does not hold such ill regard for the Dean family. You honor your grandfather well. Did you know he and Ronald were great friends when we were younger? Though in secret, of course. Much like you and Jackson." She flashed a quick grin and then released her. "Well, I'll be on my way, sugar foot. You take care now, and you let me know if my Jack gives ya any trouble." She pointed at Liz until Liz nodded. As the older woman walked away, waving and greeting others as she passed, Liz stood baffled. In a daze, she grabbed the first box of pasta she saw and hurried towards the register.

∞

As Liz pulled into the drive, Jackson climbed down a series of scaffolding platforms and walked towards her. She reached into the backseat of her SUV and grabbed a couple of paper sacks. "May I help you with those?"

She jumped, and he grabbed the first bag before it slipped from her hand. She placed a hand over her heart. "You scared me."

"Sorry about that." He began to follow her into the house and she froze at the door.

"We need to talk."

Her tone had him wincing as he was led towards the kitchen and she set her bag on the counter. He followed suit. "I'm all ears."

"I bumped into your grandmother at the grocery store." She waited for him to react, but saw nothing and only grew more frustrated. "She spoke to me."

He slid his hands into his pockets. "And?"

"*And*?" She slapped his arm. "No one is supposed to know you are working on my house, least of all your own grandmother!"

"It's a small town, Liz. People are going to find out. Besides, I told my grandmother not to say anything to anyone about it, and if she was asked, that all questions were to be referred to me."

"Well, she was not shy about it today. Who knows who could have heard her in the store."

"She promised not to cause problems with your grandmother. She knows my very job depends on the fact of my name remaining under wraps. She wouldn't jeopardize this job for me. We have nothing to worry about."

Liz rubbed her hands over her face and then sighed. "You're right. I'm sorry. I just... well, it's a bit unnerving to be approached by your grandmother's sworn enemy on the pasta aisle. I feel so..."

"So what?" he prodded.

"Traitorous. I know that sounds ridiculous, but it's how I feel. I've never had to keep a secret from my grandmother, especially one of this magnitude. If she were to find out... let's just say we would both be dead."

"I think we will be fine. Besides, you are only employing me because there is no other option."

"That sounds even worse," Liz admonished. "You are gifted at what you do, Jackson, I don't want you to discredit yourself to make me feel better. It's my dishonesty that is my burden. Your skill is evident, and even being a Dean, you deserve the job."

"Then there. It's settled. If your grandmother finds out my name, you can just explain it to her that way."

Liz reached into a grocery bag and withdrew a bag of lettuce. "Right. So easy." Her voice was dripping with sarcasm.

"Well, I better get back out there. Just wanted to let you know we should be finished with the scaffolding today."

"Already? Wow, that was quick. So what's next?"

"Tomorrow we will have the outside crew start ripping off all the exterior damage and rot with the siding while I have the interior crew begin work on your wing upstairs. I want to start up there with the add ins so that you will have a functional kitchen for when we decide to gut this one."

"Makes sense. I haven't really unpacked much upstairs knowing we would be tackling my wing of the house first, so nothing should be in the way."

"Good. We're wrapping up, so I better get out there and check things over."

"Of course." She watched as he walked towards the French doors leading to the patio. "Oh, Jackson?"

He turned.

"Anna and Ben are coming over for supper around seven. If you would like to join us, you are more than welcome." She waited patiently as she saw the idea being tossed around in his head.

"I'd love to." He nodded and walked out.

She exhaled the breath she hadn't realized she'd been holding. Perhaps Ginger Dean was right and Jackson would be a good addition to their friend group. *Tonight would tell,* she thought, as she sorted the rest of her groceries and began work on preparing her spaghetti sauce. *Tonight would tell.*

«CHAPTER FOUR»

"I can't believe you invited Jackson to supper." Anna waved as Ben walked up to the patio doors and knocked. Liz looked up as he entered. "Hey, Ben."

"Hey, Jackson just pulled up behind me."

"That's because Liz invited him to supper," Anna supplied. "Wasn't that nice of her?"

Ben, confused by his girlfriend's tone, nodded. "I guess so." He opened the doors before Jackson could knock. "Hey man, how's it going?" They shook hands.

"Good, things are good. Anna," he greeted and then turned to Liz with a bottle of wine. "Liz." He handed it to her.

"Thanks, this will go great with what we are having." She grinned as she accepted it and handed it to Ben. "Do the honors."

Saluting, Ben turned and found the bottle opener. "Looks like you guys covered good ground today," he commented over his shoulder to Jackson as he filled four wine glasses and handed them out. Liz fluffed the salad as Anna grabbed the basket of garlic bread. "Ready?" she asked. Liz nodded towards the stairs.

Jackson grabbed her glass for her and everyone followed her upstairs to her wing of the house. A small dining table sat centered in the ballroom, various boxes stacked along the walls and out of the way as she escorted them inside. "Sorry about the emptiness, but Grandmother prefers to have the dining hall downstairs to herself, so we will be dining in my quarters."

"Quarters." Anna snickered. "It always sounds so regal."

"Not nearly as glamorous as you envision." Liz waved her hand over the vast empty space.

"It will be," Jackson assured her as he eyed the space his team had marked off for her soon-to-be kitchen area.

"I leave it in your capable hands." She toasted him as Anna took the lid off of the spaghetti pot.

"Who's hungry?" Anna asked, dipping the tongs into the pot and pulling out noodles. "Oh…" her words trailed off.

"Yes, I forgot to mention that it isn't regular spaghetti." Flustered as she spotted Anna's nervous glance towards Ben, Liz quickly recovered. "I was a bit distracted at the grocery store today and grabbed penne instead of spaghetti noodles. It will still be tasty though."

Jackson caught Liz's look of uncertainty and smiled as Anna scooped him a hearty helping onto his plate. "I'm sure it's delicious. Better than the frozen dinner I planned to eat, so I thank you."

"Don't thank her yet," Ben added in a stage whisper, receiving a hit on the arm from Anna as Liz's gaze nervously made its way to Jackson's. He offered a reassuring smile as he waited for everyone else to be served. He watched as Liz took a tentative bite of her pasta and her shoulders relaxed. Everyone else followed suit, Ben offering praise as he shoveled his into his mouth.

Liz's phone rang. "I am sorry, that's my grandmother's ring tone." She pushed away from the table and fished her phone out of her purse. "Yes, Grandmother?"

Anna tilted her head towards the phone conversation as the men sat quietly. "Yes, that is Jackson's truck. I told you Anna and Ben were coming by for supper tonight…" a long pause and the murmurs of a voice on the other line had Liz placing an annoyed fist on her hip. "I invited him to supper, Grandm—" Liz suddenly hung up and walked back to the table.

"Everything okay?" Ben asked.

"Just Grandmother being nosy."

"I don't think she likes me just yet," Jackson admitted and caught the apologetic glance from Liz.

"Don't take it personally," Anna commented. "Sissy Montgomery doesn't like anyone but her own reflection."

"Annie," Ben scolded.

Liz chuckled. "Don't worry, Ben. I don't take offense. Sadly, it's true. My grandmother has always been a hard woman, but she was loving in her own way. Since Grandfather's death, however, she seems to be struggling with even liking me these days."

"She is probably still mourning." Jackson said, attempting justification.

Shrugging, Liz took a sip of her wine. "I try not to think on it, and neither should y'all. Everything is looking up now that the house is underway."

A loud crash resounded as Liz jerked around towards the doorway. "What was that?"

The men stood and walked towards the doorway and Ben opened it. No one stood on the other side. He peered down the hall and saw nothing. "Nothing out here." He shut the door.

Jackson walked towards the patio doors that led to the balcony and opened them. Checking the scaffolding surrounding the house, he shook his head. "Nothing."

Liz eased back into her chair. "That's weird. It sounded like something falling onto the floor."

"Maybe it's one of the old paintings in the hall or something," Anna suggested, sipping her wine and then taking another bite of spaghetti.

"Perhaps it's that ghost I've heard so much about," Jackson teased as he took his seat again.

Rolling her eyes, Liz offered him more garlic bread. "Don't go spreading rumors, Mr. Dean."

Anna gasped. "Elizabeth Montgomery! How dare you say the 'D' word!"

Ben laughed as Jackson's face slightly flushed. "Dangerous talk goin' on here," Ben added, rubbing his hands together in anticipation. "So you think your grandmother still doesn't know?"

"As far as I know." Liz scooted her plate towards the center of the table. "And please, let's not talk about that because I'm consumed by this overwhelming sense of guilt every time I think about it."

"You shouldn't be." Anna's voice was firm as she flipped her red hair over her shoulder. "Your grandmother needs to get over her hatred. I mean, come on! It's been 50 years since Mr. Dean rejected her. She found love, what's the big deal?"

Jackson looked stunned. "What are you talking about?"

"You don't know?" Ben asked.

"No. I have never heard of this."

Liz placed her chin in her hand and waved for Ben to continue the story. "Might as well."

Ben leaned back in his chair as he crossed his ankle over his knee. "Liz's grandmother used to have the hots for your grandfather."

"Okay now," Liz interjected. "Tell it like it happened, not some cheap version. She deserves a bit more class than that."

Ben blushed before continuing. "Sorry. So any way, back in the day your grandfather, Ronald, dated Sissy Montgomery, though then her name was—?"

"Sissy Hanson," Liz provided.

"Sissy Hanson." Ben continued. "They were young, probably eighteen or nineteen, but very much in love from all accounts we've heard. Then one day, Ginger moves to town with her family. Her father is a well-to-do banker, she's pretty, sweet, and a bit on the flirty side."

"Still is," Jackson added, earning him a small smile from Liz as Ben continued.

"She won Ronald over. His attention started to be drawn away from Sissy towards Ginger. Well, Sissy couldn't have that. She and Ronald were engaged."

"*Engaged*?" Jackson asked. "No kidding?"

"No kidding," Ben replied. "Sissy gave ol' Ron the ultimatum. Her or Ginger. He chose Ginger and ended things with Sissy right then and there. Less than a year later he married Ginger and had their first kid, your Uncle Samuel."

"So what happened with Sissy after that?" Jackson asked, pity in his voice.

"She met my grandfather on a summer vacation. She left town after the engagement of Ronald and Ginger was announced and spent the summer with her aunt in Florida. That's where she met my grandfather. He was on vacation with his family. She knew him from Quinton, of course, but they had never gotten acquainted due to her relationship with Ronald. They had a whimsical summer and came back to Quinton married and with a baby on the way," Liz finished.

"And Sissy still holds a grudge against my grandmother even though she seemed to find happiness?"

"Holding a grudge is like drinking poison, and my grandmother adds a special spoonful to her tea every morning," Liz stated. "She will never let it go, just like she has never forgiven me for breaking her crystal decanter when I was nine."

"Wow." Jackson rubbed a hand over his jaw. "That has to be a tough way to live."

"She manages, though I don't think she's ever been truly happy."

"I meant for you," he clarified, causing her navy eyes to jolt to his.

"Oh," she said quietly. "It wasn't so bad. My grandfather was amazing. And where my grandmother was hard, he was soft. He spoiled me rotten." She smiled at the memory. "She just managed to make sure I wasn't so spoiled as to be ruined for good. An equal balance."

"Still," Ben added. "I remember being terrified of her in high school. When I dropped you off after prom, you remember that?"

Liz laughed at the memory and had Jackson's brows rising. "You were prom dates?"

They both nodded. "It was awful," they both said at the same time. "Ben went with me to make Anna jealous, I went with him to try and make Marcus Andrews jealous, and all it did was get us both in trouble. Ben was late getting me home and I missed curfew. When we arrived, he walked me to the door like a gentleman, and before he could leave, Grandmother turned the hose on him. Drenched him head to toe for being a 'no good Wheeler tryin' to tarnish the Montgomery name.'" She laughed as Ben ran a hand over his embarrassed face. "And she has never forgiven me," he pointed out. "That was the day I realized I did not quite care for Sissy Montgomery and the feeling was mutual."

Anna shook her head as she laughed with them. "The good ol' days."

"For you, maybe." Ben shook his head as if trying to erase the memory.

As the friends laughed over high school memories, Jackson found himself amused and at ease. Though he did not share such a history with all of them, they seemed to welcome him into the fold. When Liz started clearing the dishes and placing them in a basket to take back downstairs, he stood to help. She waved him down. "I've got it, you relax."

"Don't go lookin' a gift horse in the mouth, Lizzy," Anna scolded.

Liz acknowledged her friend's warning with a nod. She gestured for Jackson to grab the spaghetti pot and salad bowl. "We'll meet you two on the patio downstairs. Y'all grab the wine and glasses, Jackson and I will take care of the dishes."

She led the way down the stairs back to the kitchen and unloaded the basket.

"I can wash these later," she said as she rinsed her hands.

"I don't mind helping you right now."

"No, no, no, I've got them. Besides, Ben and Anna are probably already waiting on us out there."

"What was that Anna said to you? Something about a horse's mouth."

Laughing, Liz nudged him towards the patio doors. "Never turn down a gift or nice offer," Liz explained. "But this time, I am. Come on." She opened the patio doors to find their friends waiting for them.

Anna swatted a mosquito as it landed on her ankle. "The only downside to summer is stinkin' mosquitos."

"I would say the only downside is this sweltering heat," Ben added, pulling his damp shirt away from his chest.

"August is brutal in Quinton," Liz acknowledged. "Speaking of which, you need to make sure your men have plenty of water while they work. It gets horribly hot here." She saw Jackson's nod as he sipped his wine. "Especially tomorrow. I saw on the news it was to reach triple digits tomorrow."

"Yuck," Anna complained. "I'm afraid my entire summer vacation is going to be spent indoors."

"Speaking of indoors," Liz's leading tone had Anna's right brow rising. "I plan on working up at the boutique tomorrow, want to help?"

"Depends on what you mean by help," Anna quipped.

"Peeling wall paper." Liz grimaced.

"No thanks," Anna replied. "But in all honesty, I have to run my mom up to Atlanta tomorrow, otherwise I would help you."

"No worries. I'm hoping to at least get started in there. There's a lot of work that needs to be done."

"Boutique?" Jackson asked.

"Liz plans to open up a fabulous boutique downtown in one of the abandoned buildings her grandmother owns."

"Unfortunately the only contractor I trust is busy with a big project, otherwise I would hire him to help me with the boutique building as well." Liz winked at him as she handed her empty glass to Ben to top off.

"I could come take a look at it, at least give you some ideas on what's needed. If there are some things that can be knocked out by yourself, start with those, and in my spare time I could help with the rest."

"I don't want to be a burden any more than I already am," Liz pointed out. "But I also don't want to turn down an expert opinion. I'm a bit in over my head."

"Then it's settled. How about tomorrow after I check on things here in the morning I can come by the boutique, say about 9:30?"

Liz reached forward and gripped his hand appreciatively. "Jackson, that would be amazing. Thank you." Squeezing his fingers before she slid her hand away, Jackson made a mental note for his morning schedule, finding that the more reasons he had to see Liz, the better his day looked to be.

∞

Jackson set his notepad on the remnants of the old counter top that had once served as a cash wrap. The wood was scarred from years of use and the glass display shelves had long since shattered.

It spoke of time lost as it sat covered in dust, glass, and cobwebs.

"I can tell by your face that the news is not good." Liz leaned against a shelving unit and it shifted behind her. She stumbled before catching her balance and cleared her throat, straightening her blouse as if nothing had happened. Jackson just shook his head in dread. "That shelf is definitely the least of your worries."

Defeated, Liz crossed her arms in an aggravated huff. "Seems my hopes of doing most of the work myself are going up in smoke."

"Not exactly," Jackson continued. "Looks to me like you will have your hands full clearing this place of old furniture and creatures." He fingered a fossilized beetle before tossing it to the floor. "Once that's happened, my suggestion is to do what you planned to start today and peel that wall paper. Once the walls are stripped, you can look at repairing holes as well as what treatment you want to do to the walls next. I think that gives you a good start."

"Thanks for coming to take a look at this."

"No problem. It's a beautiful building. With care and repair it could be even more so." He slid his pen behind his ear and Liz noted how his dark hair curled around it. *He was in need of a trim*, she realized, though she had to admit she liked the way the tips of his hair curled around his collar.

“I’ll see you back at the house.” He handed her a sheet of paper with his suggestions and she walked him to the door.

“I’m thankful I haven’t run you off yet.”

“It would take more than hard work to scare me off.”

“I’m starting to see that.” Smiling, she shut the door behind him and watched as he confidently climbed into his truck and pulled away from the curb.

«CHAPTER FIVE»

Pulling to the front of her family's home, Liz sat in her car and watched as various men and their equipment worked diligently to restore the once magnificent structure. What would her grandfather think about her finally moving forward with the plans they had long talked about? About the renovations she decided upon inside? About her deceiving her grandmother? She shook that thought away. Again, she reminded herself, she didn't want to think on that. It was for the best. Jackson was their best option at the moment, and if the work was to be done, then they could not be picky. Dean or no Dean. Resolute in her thinking, Liz slid from the car and made her way up to the porch. She noticed the men working hard to avoid trampling the rose bushes planted in the beds along the side of the house, and the small gesture made her resolute in her hiring decisions.

When she stepped inside, Jackson was coming down the main stairs drenched in sweat with a tool belt loosely hung around his hips. He smiled in greeting. "How'd it go today?"

"I should be asking you the same question. It's as hot as the hinges on the gates of Hades in here! Why is the air conditioning turned off?"

He shrugged. "We assumed you or your grandmother turned it off."

"You've been working in this heat *all day*?" She spun to the house intercom and pressed the button calling for the maid. The older woman appeared over the railing from the west wing of the house. "Yes, Ms. Lizbeth?"

"Why is the air turned off?" She saw the older woman shake her head in dismay as she began heading towards the stairwell, but Sissy Montgomery stepped out of the west wing with pride and anger. "Leave it to me, Mitzy," she called to the woman. "I need to have a word with my granddaughter." The sound of her cane on the stairs sent the childhood shimmer of dread seeping down Liz's spine. She looked to Jackson with regret. "You might want to head on outside or upstairs. This looks like it will take a while."

He lightly brushed his fingers over her hand. “If you need me—” His offer was cut off as Sissy reached the bottom stair. “The boy stays,” she ordered and motioned towards the parlor. Liz and Jackson shared a glance before walking into the small sitting room.

“Lizbeth, I am appalled at you,” she stated, as she sat in her chair.

Liz stood silent as she waited for whatever crime she committed to surface. Sissy Montgomery pointed a finger at Jackson. “To bring that boy into my house under false pretenses—”

Liz’s stomach filled with a sinking weight.

“Mrs. Montgomery, we can explain—” Jackson began and was silenced with a death glare.

“If you wished to date the boy, you did not have to hire him in order for me to get used to him,” Sissy stated and waved a hand for them to sit before her. They slowly eased to a small chaise. “I’m sorry?” Liz asked, completely taken aback at her grandmother’s accusation.

Sissy smiled and then turned towards Jackson. “My granddaughter has never liked me knowing who has her interest ever since I sprayed that Wheeler boy with the hose in high school.”

“For the record, Ben and I never dated,” Liz pointed out.

"He was late." Sissy barked with a sharp look of disapproval. "And you should have known better. Just as you should have known better now. Why in the world would you devise such an elaborate ploy to get your boyfriend hired as the contractor? We met with four different ones for crying out loud. If I had known you planned to hire this young man all along, I would have made sure you had not wasted my time."

"Grandmother—" Liz tried to interrupt but Sissy held up her hand.

"Now," Sissy shifted to the edge of her seat, her back regally straight and her ankles crossed. "Now that we are all on the same page, young man, you will come to dinner tonight."

Jackson sat speechless, unsure of what was to be said. Thankfully, Liz saved him. "Grandmother, listen to me. First off, Jackson and I are not dating. We just met the day he came to survey the house and I did not try to pull a fast one over on you. Second, why is the air conditioning turned off? Jackson and his men are about to melt."

Sissy crossed her arms. "I was testing his stuff."

"*What*?" Liz shook her head and placed her fingers to her forehead. "What do you mean?"

"Well, I wanted to see if he could sweat it out without complaint. My granddaughter needs a man who is not afraid to work hard."

"Grandmother," Liz scolded underneath her breath. "Jackson, I am terribly sorry about all this."

"Don't apologize to the boy, he passed." Sissy nodded her approval. "Not one complaint, all day."

Jackson's lips twitched into a slow smile as he stood. "I am glad to have passed your test, Mrs. Montgomery, but I really must be getting back. I am sorry if there was any misunderstanding."

"Not on my end," Sissy added.

"Of course," Jackson amended as he shot Liz an apologetic look. She blushed at the misunderstanding and he eased his way back outside.

"Grandmother I cannot believe you accused me of dating the contractor. And in front of him, no less! What made you think such a thing?"

"Don't take that tone with me, girl. I've seen the way you two look at each other. And the stolen moments together."

Liz bolted to her feet. "*What*?" Hands widespread, she rubbed them over her face. "This is insane. You are insane! He's working for us!"

“Then why was his truck here last night?” Sissy asked.

“Because I asked him to supper,” Liz challenged. “He and Ben are friends. Anna was going to be here too, so I thought it would be a nice gesture to ask Jackson as well.”

“To ask your contractor to dinner?” Sissy asked skeptically.

Groaning in frustration, Liz reached for her purse. “This conversation is ridiculous. I’m heading upstairs.”

“You dare not walk away from me, young lady. Not while I’m talking to you!” Sissy’s voice rose as she turned and saw Liz’s back snap straight.

“You are being unreasonable and ridiculous, Grandmother. I am not dating Jackson Dean! I hired him because he is the only contract—”

“*Dean*?” Her grandmother stood and her face flushed red as anger engulfed her small frame. “That boy is a Dean?”

Liz’s shoulders dropped as she realized she let the name slip. “He is.” Her voice was quiet, resigned, as she watched her grandmother.

“How dare you bring a Dean into my home!” Anger and disgust flooded her grandmother’s voice.

"Grandmother," Liz held out her hand to calm the rage she felt clear across the room.

"They are a despicable breed and I will not have him step one more toe into this house if it's the last thing I do." Sissy slammed her cane into the floor.

Liz cringed when she heard the front door open and Jackson poked his head inside. "Hey Liz, I wanted to run something by you out here."

"Get out!" Sissy yelled, her gnarled finger pointing at him. She quickly cleared the room and headed straight towards him, her cane raised as if she could shove him off the steps. "Get out of my house!" she yelled. Liz caught her around the shoulders before she tore through a surprised Jackson.

Liz caught his concerned gaze and felt tears behind her eyes. She shook her head as he took one step forward. "You should wait outside," she whispered, before her grandmother tore from her touch and banged her cane on the floor with a final shout. "No Dean is allowed on this property! Leave!"

Jackson eyed the woman with pity as he shook his head and stepped out onto the front porch and the heavy door swung closed with a bang.

Liz sank to the bottom stair as her grandmother turned.

"I can't abide to look at ya," Sissy spat.

"That makes two of us," Liz mumbled as she stood to her feet.

Sissy's eyes widened. "Watch yourself, girl. You have no right to speak to me that way after you've lied to me. You know the rules of this house. No Dean is allowed to step foot here."

"Jackson is different, Grandmother."

"They're all the same!"

"You are being irrational." Liz tried to remain calm as her insides burned with fury. "Ten minutes ago you were pleased with the notion of me dating him, and now you want him off the property?"

Sissy shook her head. "God forbid you ever understand the depth of hurt Ronald Dean did to me. Or the series of Deans wronging Montgomerys before him."

"You're right, Grandmother, I hope that I never have to experience the loss of love that you have, but you have loved since then. Grandfather was a good man. He loved you and cared for you. This is his house too. And Jackson—"

"Is a Dean." Sissy's words were final as she turned to make her way up the steps.

"He will continue working on the house," Liz said to her retreating back. She watched as her grandmother paused a moment to listen. "Your prejudice to his family will have to be shelved for the duration of this renovation. Thanks to all the ghost stories spreading around town, he's the best choice we have right now. I'm sorry I misled you. But this is the very reason I did what I did."

Sissy turned and shook her head. "Then he will be made as uncomfortable as possible until he leaves on his own. That's what Deans are best at any way." Shaking her head in disgust, Sissy made her way back to her wing of the house.

∞

Jackson did indeed keep working on the house, though his team met with disaster after disaster. First there was rot damage on the exterior of house, which then led to the discovery of rot damage on the inside as well. Then as he began the work of tying in the plumbing, he discovered corrosion in the pipes and he had to break the bad news to Liz about replacing it all. He ran a hand through his hair as he dreaded that conversation. He had rarely seen Liz throughout the week, and he never saw Sissy Montgomery. He glanced up as the patio doors opened and Liz walked out carrying two glasses of lemonade. "Thought you could use this." She slid him a glass as she sat opposite him, her gaze perusing the blueprints spread before him on the patio table. "You look frustrated." She took a sip of her drink and waited for him to do the same. When he did, he sighed. “Thanks for this.”

“Don’t mention it. Now tell me why your face lacks its usual smile.”

“I’m afraid I have bad news.”

“Okay. Lay it on me.” Liz leaned forward in her chair and saw his eyes examine his notes. “There’s an extensive amount of rot damage on the exterior of the house.”

“We figured there would be,” Liz added without a problem. “What’s the big issue you’re scared to tell me?”

His mouth quirked to the right as he fought back a grin. “Since you see right through me,” he began. “The plumbing.”

“What’s wrong with the plumbing?” She frowned as she leaned back in her chair and studied him.

“It needs to be replaced.”

“Well, that doesn’t sound too bad.” Liz’s smile faded as she saw him shake his head. “Okay, it’s bad. How bad?”

“It needs to be replaced throughout the entire house.”

“Wait, what? The *entire* house? Why?”

He exhaled a long breath before waving a hand over the blueprints. "No doubt the copper plumbing has lasted as long as it has due to the water's pH level being higher than the norm. But over time corrosion still happens. I'd gather there hasn't been new piping installed since around the 1930s. I noticed several places where there's been some water leaks, but you can kiss a new kitchen or bathroom goodbye unless you replace the plumbing. Plus, in order for codes to be met, it's going to have to happen."

"I see." Liz popped her lips as she ran everything he said through her head. "So how expensive is this looking?"

He shrugged his shoulders. "I was working on an estimate right now actually."

"You know what, it doesn't matter. If it has to be done, it has to be done. Just get me the numbers and add it to the overall cost for the east wing."

"I can come up with a few options for you, Liz."

"Okay. How quick can you do that? I'm assuming this is a decision that needs to be made quickly?"

"I can have it for you by the end of the day. It's what I'm working on now."

"Good." She pushed up off the chair and grabbed her glass. "I will leave you to it then."

Jackson shifted to look up at her. "Things okay with your grandmother?" He saw the regret in her eyes as she shook her head.

"She's still not speaking to me. And she's mad as a hornet that I turned the air conditioning back on for you and your team. But that's okay. I can handle Sissy Montgomery. If she thinks petty games of turning off the air are going to convince me to fire you, she has another thing coming."

Jackson looked down at his papers. "Look, Liz, I could try and find another contractor for you. One I trust, if need be. I don't want to come between you and your grandmother."

"You're not."

"Um, yes, I am. She hates me, and because you hired me, she is now upset with you. I don't like being the cause of it."

"It's not you she hates."

"It's my family. Same thing."

"But her reasons are uncalled for. Well, okay, they are a little justifiable, I mean, her having her feelings hurt and all. The holding a grudge for 50 years is not. Your family has moved on and so should she."

"Just promise me that if things get worse you'll tell me, and we can look at other contractors for you?"

"Jackson," Liz pinched the bridge of her nose as she tried to be patient. "Look, I have had multiple contractors come out here and they were scared off due to all the weird things that happened, or they heard bad things about the house and refused to even look at it. The odds of finding another contractor, especially after the work has commenced, is slim to none. I want you, and I will have you."

His lips twitched and she flushed. "I mean, as my contractor." She waved her hands to ward off any confusion.

"I knew what you meant, Liz." He laughed as she ran a hand over her face.

"Right. Well, I should get back and let you work. Thanks for letting me know about the plumbing."

"Should I tell your grandmother?" he asked.

She shook her head. "No. She won't speak with you."

"Or you," he pointed out again.

"Yes, but I can leave her a report with Mitzy or something."

He shook his head. "I don't like this, Liz."

"I know. And I'm sorry it's made you uncomfortable here."

"I'm fine. I don't like it for you. Sissy doesn't know me. She's *your* grandmother. You're family. I don't like how she's treating you over this."

"She'll come around. It's just given me a new project to work on."

"And what project is that? The boutique?"

"Ugh, no. That's a whole other can of worms." She crossed her arms as she leaned against the doorframe. "My latest project is to remind her of how wonderful my grandfather was and how much they loved one another. Hopefully by remembering him, her hatred for your family will ease."

"Did it while your grandfather was still alive?"

Liz shook her head. "No, not really. She wasn't as bad, but her underlying feelings were still there. But they weren't as strong. She's just... lost, I'm afraid. My grandfather balanced her. He was good for her. And she's lost that other half. I imagine it would throw anyone out of sorts. Sissy Montgomery isn't just anyone though, so I've got my work cut out for me."

"She's blessed to have you in her life and to worry so much for her."

Liz rolled her eyes on a laugh. "Try explaining that to her."

"I don't have to. She knows." His confidence had her eyes watering, but she turned to head back into the house so he could not see.

"Thanks," she muttered. "I'll let you get back to work."

He watched as she made her way through the kitchen and towards the main part of the house wondering how she managed to stay positive about her grandmother's potential transformation. Looking at the messy plumbing issue before him, Jackson realized he would much rather handle that project than Sissy Montgomery.

«CHAPTER SIX»

Anna dumped a dustpan full of glass and bug skeletons into the trashcan as she turned towards Liz. “So she still hasn’t spoken to you?”

Liz shook her head. “Well, I take that back,” she commented. “She started to mention something to me about her bridge club yesterday but then stopped herself realizing it was me she was speaking to instead of Mitzy.”

“Seriously?” Anna asked, her hand on her hip and a look of irritation etched on her pretty face. “That woman is as stubborn as a mule, and not in a good way. You’re her granddaughter, whom she *raised*! Why would she waste such precious time with you by being mad? Especially since you just lost your grandfather. Doesn’t she know you’re still grieving? Doesn't she know you don't want to lose both grandparents?"

Liz paused and waved her finger at her friend as if she just realized something. "You are exactly right."

"I know I am," Anna stated matter-of-factly.

"She does know I'm still grieving and she is still acting like this."

"Exactly." Anna nodded with enthusiasm as she resumed pushing the broom across the floor.

"I can only imagine how badly she is still grieving and how it must pain her that I'm being so defiant."

Anna paused in her sweeping. "Wait, what?"

"Think about it," Liz explained. "I miss Grandfather so much, but it's like I told Jackson the other day, she just lost the love of her life. I can't imagine how painful it must be to wake up without him each day. And then she has a granddaughter deliberately deceiving her in the second most hurtful thing she could do to her by hiring a Dean under her nose."

"And what would be the first most hurtful?"

"If I married a Dean."

"Right, of course, carry on." Anna waved for her to continue and Liz smiled.

"Right. So my plans to remind her about grandfather will mean nothing if I don't also remind her that I lost him too. That we share in that pain together and that the last thing I would ever want is to lose her too or make her even more unhappy."

"But haven't you tried that already?" Anna asked.

"Yes, but not hard enough. I've avoided her all week. I've played to her game. Well, no more." Liz cut her hand through the air in finality. "Today when I get home I'm going to march up to her wing of the house and force her to speak to me. And even if she just sits there with that pinched expression of disapproval, I'm going to break through with kindness and love. Yep, that's what I'm gonna do." Liz paced back and forth as she spoke, her tangent causing her southern drawl to be more pronounced and Anna smiled at the fire she witnessed in her friend's disposition.

"You go girl," she chanted in encouragement. Liz never stopped pacing as she continued ranting and waving her hands as she spoke.

"I am. And Sissy Montgomery will have met her match! She will begin to understand why I acted the way I did, why I hired Jackson, and even as a Dean, he is the best contractor this side of the Mississippi!"

Slow claps echoing off the walls had her halting, and had Anna spinning around towards the doorway in surprise. Jackson and Ben stood there with pleased smiles as Liz flushed from head to toe.

"Liz Montgomery, welcome back." Ben stepped forward and nudged her shoulder. "That was a pretty passionate speech."

Liz tried to hide her embarrassment at being overheard. "Well, it is all true and the way I feel, no sense in keepin' it trapped inside."

"I couldn't agree more." Ben winked at her as he made his way towards Anna and lowered into a princely bow. "Why, my Cinderella, shall I rescue you from this dungeon and sweep you away to supper?"

Playing her part well, Anna swiftly removed the bandana from her hair and graciously extended her hand to him. "Why of course," her sweet drawl played upon and paired with batting eyelashes. She grinned at him as he stood and linked his fingers with hers. "We're getting food. See you two later." He took the broom from Anna's other hand and began escorting her out the door. Liz watched them a moment through the dingy windows as they laughed and nuzzled their way up the street towards the small café.

"They're a good couple," Jackson said, echoing the sentiments floating in her head.

Nodding, she grabbed her own broom again and began sweeping. "So what brought you two boys by?"

Slipping his hands into his pockets, he watched her. "Wanted to pick up a few supplies from the hardware store. Ben mentioned the two of you working over here, so we thought we would stop by and see how it's going." He looked around the room. "You've come a long way."

"You were right in your assessment. It's taken me a week and a half just to get the building cleared out and now cleaned."

"It always takes more time than planned."

"How's the plumbing coming?"

"It's coming," he said, his tired tone causing her to glance up and catch his exhausted expression.

"You look beat."

A smirk tilted his lips. "Thanks."

She blushed. "I didn't mean that to sound rude."

"It didn't."

"Have you eaten supper?"

His brows rose slightly and she turned back to sweeping to avoid him seeing the blush to her cheeks again.

"Have you?" he countered.

"Not yet. Mitzy called me earlier and said she would be leaving supper warming for me in the oven. That's Grandmother's doing."

"That Mitzy would leave you food?"

Liz nodded with a small smile. "Our feud is starting to wear on her. Which is a good thing."

"I don't understand."

"Mitzy doesn't cook for us. She tends to the house and such, but at the end of every day she has her own separate living quarters or apartment within the house. She is not our cook. Either Grandmother or I cook each day. The fact that Grandmother cooked and Mitzy is leaving something in the oven means Grandmother told her to do so, otherwise the kitchen would be completely cleaned before Mitzy retired for the evening."

"Mitzy could just be looking out for you," he suggested.

Liz shook her head. "No." She pushed the broom harder across the floor as she worked to tidy up the large space. "I believe it was my grandmother. I choose to believe she is softening."

"I see." He reached out and took the broom from her hands and leaned it against the wall. "For your sake, I hope she is."

"So how 'bout it? Want to join me for whatever lies in the oven?" Liz asked.

He stood a moment just studying her and she began to fidget, first by removing her own bandana from her hair and then wiping it over her face. "I would," he fished into his pocket for his keys, "but I don't live too far from here, and as you pointed out earlier, I'm exhausted."

"Oh… of course." Feeling a bit self-conscious, she turned towards the wall housing a row of collapsing cabinets and retrieved her purse. "I understand."

"Perhaps a rain check though?" he asked, his tone full of regret.

She nodded. "Of course." Forcing a polite smile, she gestured towards the door. "I think I'm done for today."

When they stepped outside, laughter from the café's outdoor patio up the street filtered towards them. Liz locked the door and dropped her keychain back into her purse. "I guess I will see you tomorrow then. Possibly."

He pointed up the street towards her car. "I'll walk with you."

She noticed his truck the opposite direction. "You don't have to do that. I know you're tired, and you're parked that way. I'll be fine."

Instead of responding he continued walking beside her towards her own car. When she clicked the keys to unlock it, he reached for her door and opened it. "Thank you."

"Be careful heading home, Liz, and enjoy that meal your grandmother made you." He winked at her as she slid inside and he shut the door. Tapping his knuckles against her window in farewell, she watched him jog back across the street and make his way towards his truck at a leisurely pace with his hands tucked in his pockets. Sighing, she cranked the engine and headed towards home.

∞

"Yoo hoo! Jack Dear!"

Jackson finished his conversation with the plumber before he turned and found his grandmother standing by her car waving enthusiastically for him to go to her.

"What in the world?" he mumbled, praying Sissy Montgomery did not come out of her home and see Ginger Dean on her property. He hurried over and lifted the cap off his head to wipe the sweat off his forehead before replacing it. "Honey, what are you doing here? You know you can't be here." His tone held worry and warning as she lightly patted his arm.

"Don't fret Jack, I'm keepin' my distance." She smiled as she shielded her eyes from the sun as she looked up at him. "My goodness sugar bean, you look too hot. You stayin' hydrated?"

"Yes, now will you please tell me why you are here so you can leave?" He tried to lightly nudge her back towards her car, but she stood her ground by implanting her sharp heels into the grass.

"Stop shovin' on me, Jackson. I am fine. Ain't nobody goin' to see me out here. Now calm down." She slapped away his hand as he tried reaching for her again. "I just happened to be drivin' by and thought I'd stop in on ya' and see how the house was comin' along."

"Oh really?" he asked, doubt evident in his voice.

She planted a hand on her chest. "Cross my heart."

"Well then, as you can see, it is a work in progress. Now can you please leave before Sissy Montgomery sees you here?"

"Oh, now that ol' bat isn't goin' to come shoo me away, don't you worry. Besides, you are my grandson and I don't trust her with you. I still don't understand what made her change her mind about lettin' you fix her house."

"Liz. Liz has been the one to help me keep this job. And right now, you're the one who is going to cause me to lose it."

"Alright, alright." She waved her hands in surrender, but as she was about to turn and leave Liz stepped out onto the porch. "Oh look! There's Liz now!" She stepped from around Jackson and waved. "Elizabeth! Elizabeth!"

Jackson ran a hand over his jaw stubble and then over the back of his neck as he saw the shock pass over Liz's face and her hurried steps towards them. "Mrs. Dean, how nice to see you. What brings you by?"

Beaming, Ginger grabbed Jackson's bicep. "Why my handsome grandson, of course."

"I see." Liz tried to offer a kind smile, but she felt her temper rising. *Why would this woman dare step foot here knowing Jackson and I fight tooth and nail to try and appease Grandmother as much as possible?*

"Honey was just leaving," Jackson explained, motioning towards his grandmother's car.

"Honey?" Liz asked.

Ginger grinned and while linking her arm with Jackson's, lightly laid her head against his shoulder. "That's what my grandkids call me. See, Ronald calls me honey bee, and the kids just took to it like, well, like flies to honey." She giggled. "I've been called Honey as a nickname ever since, instead of Grandma or Grandmother or Nanna. I think it's better, don't you? Plus, I am as sweet as honey." She winked as her words dripped with charm and though Liz smiled, she couldn't help but notice Ginger's continual glances towards the house.

"That's a sweet story. If you do not mind, I was hoping to steal Jackson for a moment."

"Oh," Ginger released her hold on her grandson and nudged him towards Liz. "I don't mind at all. Steal away." She winked at Liz again. "I should jet on home any way. I've much to do before company comes callin'. Jack, I'll see you Friday now. Don't forget." She wagged her finger at him until he nodded.

"Yes ma'am."

She slid into her car. "You know, Jack, you should invite Elizabeth." With a wave, she backed out of the drive and turned with more force than necessary and left a cloud of dust and the sounds and smells of burnt rubber in her wake.

"She's a bit of a Duke behind the wheel." Jackson shook his head as Liz's sharp blue eyes followed his grandmother's car down the road until it was out of sight.

"Daisy Duke or not, I think we can both agree that she does not need to stop by the house," Liz warned. "She's kind and everything, don't get me wrong, but if my grandm—"

"I know, I warned her." He interrupted. "I'm sorry she did. I still have no idea what her true intentions were, but something tells me they were more for a show of some sort. However, she did remind me about Friday, and I am sure that was something on her to-do list."

"What's Friday?" Liz asked and then quickly apologized. "I am so sorry, that is none of my business."

"Technically it is. She did invite you. So what are you doing Friday?" he asked, surprising her.

"Not sure," she answered warily making him laugh.

"Up for a barbeque?"

"Where?"

"Honey's place."

"At your grandparent's home?" Liz's eyes widened before she shook her head. "I don't think that would be a good idea. I'm a Montgomery."

"Yeah, but my family doesn't hate you like yours hates me." He trailed off the end of his sentence realizing how his words must have sounded. "Yikes, that sounded better in my head. I didn't mean it to sound harsh."

"No worries. I'll think about it. Friday, I mean."

"Good. I'd like it if you came."

They stood and watched as construction continued underway around the house, the buzz of activity sending echoes of hammers and saws enveloping the property. Clearing her throat, Liz spoke. "I, um, came out here to talk to you about the plumbing."

"Oh, right. What about it?" he asked, motioning towards the house.

"I saw you talking with the plumber. I was just wanting an ETA on completion."

"Oh." Jackson ran a hand over his jaw. "Probably a couple of weeks. I need to ask you where some of your secret passage ways are so that maybe I can avoid ripping out walls if possible."

"Alright." As she looked over her notes, a loud crash sounded and glass shattered out of a second story window and two men on the scaffolding shielded themselves from the outpouring shards. Jackson took off at a sprint, followed by Liz.

"What *happened*?" he barked, looking up at his men. They slowly stood and dusted off their clothes. One of them reached down and held up a metal urn. "This came at us."

Liz gasped. "Through the window?" She reached up and one man walked it down the scaffolding and handed it to her."

“Yes ma’am.”

“Did someone throw this?” she asked, her eyes hard.

“No ma’am,” he replied. “In all honesty, I didn’t see anyone in the room. At least, I don’t think there was.”

Jackson took the urn from Liz’s hands and looked it over. “It had to come out of the room somehow,” he stated, and Liz acknowledged several worried looks from his crew.

“Oh come on now, please tell me you men are not scared of imaginary ghosts. I grew up in this house and have never encountered any ghosts or spirits,” Liz assured them.

Jackson handed the urn back to Liz. “Sorry about the window, Liz.”

“Just add it to the list of everything else that needs fixing.” Liz waved her hand and walked away, carrying the urn delicately in her hands.

“Look Boss, we didn’t see anybody in the room.”

Jackson slapped his crewmen on the back with a laugh. “Then I guess you better get comfortable working with a ghost.” The men exchanged worried looks as Jackson left them to go back to his work.

«CHAPTER SEVEN»

The creaks and groans had been replaced by drills and hammers working their way through the east wing. Liz rolled over in the guest bed and found herself staring into the red face of the clock blaring 7 am. Groaning, she flipped the covers back. *Why were they here so early,* she wondered?

As she made her way towards the small bath across the hall, she reminded herself to be grateful for the hard work Jackson's team exhibited and that were it not for that hard work she would be living in the guest room from here on out. She couldn't wait for the east wing to be complete, and after it was, then the work could begin on the west wing. Her grandmother's wing of the house was more primitive than even Liz's, but Liz had promised her grandfather that she would see to it that Sissy Montgomery would want for nothing when it came to this house. And she aimed to keep her promise. She showered, and after applying a light veil of makeup, made her way to the kitchen. She paused in the doorway as she studied her grandmother sitting at the small dinette table by the patio doors. The morning sun had just started peeking through the clouds and one lone ray shone through the glass doors and settled upon the center of the table. Her grandmother worked the morning crossword puzzle, something Liz remembered her doing every single day with her grandfather, and their knack for such puzzles amazed her. Years of practice, she reminded herself, as she watched a small smile tip her grandmother's lips as she eagerly penciled in an answer. Her hands shook slightly as she wrote and Liz saddened a moment as she thought back to those same hands being strong and capable. Strong enough to lift and carry her on her hip, even at seven years old. Capable enough to tend her flowerbeds and gardens, knit, and even catch a softball or two when Liz was in high school. Now, those beautiful hands were weathered with age, the weakening of resilience due only to the passing of time. *They were still beautiful,* she thought, *just in a different light.* "Looks like it will be a beautiful day," Liz announced, walking into the room.

Sissy jumped slightly in her chair at the sound and watched as Liz acted as if there were no problems lurking between the two of them. Sissy studied Liz as her granddaughter poured a mug of coffee and added her usual squirt of honey and cream. *Just like her grandfather.* Sissy's heart sighed at the memory.

"Seems Jackson and his crew have had an early start this morning," Liz continued. "I know he planned on starting the installation of the new plumbing. I'm supposed to show him several wet walls today. He's hoping the replacement will be easy, but warned me that with a house this old, problems tend to pop up all the time."

Sissy said nothing as Liz eased into a seat across from her. "How far are you?" she asked, leaning over the paper and perusing Sissy's work. Her eyes scanned the puzzle before she leaned back in her chair and took a sip of her coffee. Meeting Sissy's eyes she said, "I will never know how you and Grandfather completed those every morning. I tend to only fill in three or four blanks before I mess up or give up." She chuckled as she turned to look out the doors. "They'll be replacing the upstairs window today. I'm not sure if Mitzy told you or not, but someone threw an urn out the window yesterday while Jackson's men were working on the other side of it. They didn't see anyone throw it, but the window shattered to pieces."

Liz took another sip and eyed her grandmother over the lip of her mug. "Any ideas?" Not waiting for an answer, knowing she wouldn't receive one, Liz changed the subject. "I plan on meeting with Jackson this morning on the patio. You're welcome to join us. After that, I plan on working up at the boutique for the rest of the day. You would be amazed at all the work Anna and I have accomplished up there. We just recently emptied the building and cleaned it from top to bottom. You never told me the floors were so beautiful. The black and white tiles are absolutely stunning. I can't wait for you to see them." Seeing Jackson through the doors, she smiled. "I guess that's my cue." She turned towards her grandmother once more. "I hope you have a good day, Grandmother. I love you." She stood and opened the French doors to the morning humidity and felt as if she might possibly have shown her grandmother a maturity she didn't even know she possessed. "Good morning."

Jackson turned from talking with one of his men and a wide smile spread over his face. "Hey you, we didn't wake you did we?"

She shrugged. "I'm okay that you did. It means the house is coming along. Coffee?" She motioned over her shoulder and Jackson spied Sissy sitting at the table watching them. He nodded politely in her direction but then shook his head. "No, that's okay. I think I've had about four cups already and am having trouble keeping still."

She grinned as he shoved his pen behind his ear; a habit, she realized, that he mindlessly did as one pen already resided there and another hid behind his other ear. "So, want me to walk you through today?" he asked.

"Yes, please. I'm ready." Liz pulled out a chair at the patio table, making certain she left the patio doors open so that her grandmother could hear their conversation and feel included, even if she pretended not to be.

"Well, it is as we feared. We cannot tie into the old plumbing due to corrosion. The connections are bad. We've backed our way up all the way to the outside fitting and water source and there's really no way to keep what's already here."

"So what does that mean?" Liz asked.

"Unfortunately it means we are going to have to tear into some walls and possibly floors. However, I'm hoping our little quest today through some of your secret passages will give us exposed piping there instead of hidden within the walls. That would prevent us from having to tear into anything."

"I see. Well, it needs to be done."

"Exactly," he agreed. "So we are going to do what we can today in finding pipe paths and then I can let you know the extent of what we have to rip out wall-wise."

"Sounds good."

"Man, if only all my customers were this agreeable," he teased, as he stood. "My days and projects would go by so much faster and smoother."

She walked with him a ways and paused. "Did you hear that?" She gripped his arm and had him stopping.

"That's just a sander," he explained and began walking again.

She heard the sound once more and stopped him. "There it is again. Do you hear it?" She strained towards the edge of the house and began walking in the direction of the sound.

"I hear it now, what is that?"

"Sounds like a person or animal is trapped under the house. Is anyone from your crew under there?"

"I sure hope not." Jackson hurried towards the opening of the crawl space leading underneath the old pier and beam house. The noise was louder, but he couldn't see what or where it was coming from.

"Bill, you have any idea what's making that noise?"

A man in his late forties walked towards them and brushed a handkerchief over his face. "No sir. Just thought it was one of the guys playing a ghost trick. Several of them have been doing that since the window incident. Want me to check it out?" he asked.

"No, that's okay. I will. Thanks." Jackson reached for a flashlight from the nearest toolbox and got on his hands and knees. Liz squatted beside him. "You're going in there?" she asked, nervous for him as he swiped away spider webs lining the entrance.

"Yep."

"There's no telling what's underneath there, Jackson. It could be a wild animal. With rabies. Or fangs. Or something."

He laughed as he turned his head towards her. "Fangs?"

She shrugged, her look of pure terror and innocence making his heart squeeze just a bit. He reached over and squeezed her hand. "I'll be fine. Thanks for worrying about fangs though." She shoved his shoulder as he laughed and watched as he slowly started crawling into the dark space.

∞

He followed the sounds of soft whimpers and scratches, the rays from his flashlight bouncing off of old beams that he realized had stood under the house for centuries. He brushed his hand over one as if the light touch could connect him with the past. It awed him that construction and history could combine and create such a house. A house that had withstood some of America's darkest hours. He nudged onward on his belly, pulling himself forward in an army crawl until he came to a narrow passage. He jumped and then let out a nervous laugh at himself for jumping over a spider that trekked across the back of his hand. "Get it together, Dean," he whispered to himself, as he gripped forward and instead of sodden earth, his hand pulled back a small shoe. He dropped it instantly, terrified what he might find before him as he realized the shoe was the size of a child's foot or a petite woman. The style of leather soles and torn fabric top indicated it was old. How old, he didn't know, but he decided to slip it into his pocket and ask Liz. He ventured further down the narrow path and stopped as his flashlight landed on a pile of fur. The heavy breaths of the animal rising and falling as it scratched its front paws into the ground. A dog. He exhaled a long breath, not realizing he had been holding onto one as he thanked his lucky stars there wasn't a body to match the shoe. He moved forward and gently ran his hand over the mutt and pulled back with blood on his hand. "Hey now, hey now," he shushed to the dog as he shifted his light to see what had caused the dog's injury. His eyes widened as the beam swept across two small and slimy canines. "Babies," he whispered. "You're having babies, sweetheart." He smiled as he rubbed the momma's head and started to scoot back. "Hang on little momma, I'm going to get some help for you." He elbowed and shifted his way towards the opening. "Liz!" he called, not fully exiting the crawl space.

"Yes." She was right there eagerly waiting on him and nervously winding her hands as she knelt down on her knees to peer inside.

"We need a box."

"Oh no, what is it?"

He heard the fear in her voice.

"Do you by chance have a dog?"

"A dog?" She looked confused. "No."

"Well, there is a dog under your house and she's having puppies."

"*Puppies*?" Liz exclaimed with a smile. She patted his calf so he would know she heard him. "A box. I'm on it." She watched as he began crawling back inside.

Liz hopped to her feet and hurried towards the dump trailer and scrounged around until she found a decent sized cardboard box. She then rushed into the house, passed a surprised Sissy, and darted back out with towels and a blanket. "Bill! Bill!" she called in a frantic voice; Jackson's crewman stepped forward. "Everything alright, Ms. Montgomery?"

"I need a flashlight. Do you have an extra?"

"Yes ma'am." He led her to his work truck and fished around in the tool chest on the bed. He handed her the flashlight. "Everything okay?"

"We have puppies!" she exclaimed, rushing towards the crawl space and dropping to her knees. She flicked on the flashlight and began crawling under the house.

∞

Liz followed the sounds of Jackson's voice attempting to soothe the dog as she continued to labor. *It was sweet to see him like this,* she thought. *A big, tough man lying on his stomach underneath an old house tending so gently with an innocent animal.* Her flashlight found his shoes and she tapped one of his feet. He jolted and she bit back a laugh. "Liz?" he asked, as his flashlight grazed her face. "What are you doing under here?"

"I came to help her. How many puppies do we have?"

"Looks like four."

"Four." The wonder in her tone made him smile. "How many do you think she'll have?"

"Hard to say. She's still laboring though." He stroked a hand over the animal's side. "She's skinny, so I would say she is a stray or someone dumped her off nearby."

"Oh poor thing." Liz tried to scoot closer but the space was too narrow. Jackson shifted onto his side and shared as much space as he could. Liz weaseled her way closer, their bodies brushing as she settled into place. Her hand reached forward and she stroked the momma dog's head. "Oh sweet girl, I'm so sorry you are hurting. You are not alone now," she whispered, as she continued petting the dog. She smiled at Jackson and realized how close their faces were. "I'm sorry, I just couldn't wait outside."

Smiling, he turned back to the dog. "It's no big deal. Though I do wish she hadn't chosen the farthest nook under the house to have her puppies. She could have chosen a spot near the opening of the crawl space."

Liz scoffed in mock horror, "Now Jackson Dean, that would give a lady absolutely no privacy."

"Right, of course, why did I not think about her privacy... a dog's privacy?"

Liz tapped his hand in a playful swat, though it was more of a squeeze due to their close proximity.

"You think she's in terrible pain?" Liz asked, her voice drenched with sympathy. "Should we get her out of here and take her to the veterinarian?"

Jackson chuckled, "She's fine, Liz. She's a dog. She doesn't know any other way of having puppies than what she's doing. And a vet is just going to be doing exactly what we are."

"Seems a bit unfair."

"What?" he asked.

"That we can have babies with drugs or methods that reduce our pain and she has to experience it all."

Jackson didn't respond. In his mind he thought, *It's just a dog,* but Liz's compassionate heart had him holding his tongue. She watched the dog with childlike wonder as if she'd never seen such an event. *Then again, she may never have,* he realized.

"Boss? *Boss*?" Bill's voice echoed under the house and Jackson met Liz's gaze.

"What's up, Bill?" he called back.

"We have a bit of a situation out here! Need ya' to come and take a look!"

"On my way!" Jackson looked to Liz. "I'll be back."

"Take your time. I'll stay with her."

He started to shift backwards and Liz moved to try and give him more space, but as he slipped away, their arms and legs began to tangle.

"Okay, this is tight." He bumped his elbow against a beam. "Ouch."

"You okay?" Liz asked, as she tried to navigate her flash light beam towards him, but instead shined it right into his eyes. She winced as he groaned and a laugh slipped from her lips. "Sorry."

His free hand moved her light away from his face as he now saw spots in his vision. Lowering his head, his nose bumped with Liz's and he heard her gasp. He froze, not sure what the proper protocol was in such a situation. "Sorry, Liz, excuse all this." He slid his hand around her waist and she struggled for a moment until she realized what he was doing. He quickly shifted her off her side and to her back so that he could lift up onto both arms and hover over her. From there, he began to scoot backwards with more agility and more crawl space.

"You good?" she called, as she felt him clear her ankles.

"I'm free." He flicked his flashlight towards her. "I'll be back as soon as I can to check on you two." He saw her nod.

"Never thought I'd have to work this hard to free myself from a woman." His sarcasm made her laugh and with a final wave in her direction, he disappeared in the darkness beyond the beam of her flashlight.

«CHAPTER EIGHT»

Jackson wrapped up his conversation with the electrician and cringed thinking of how he would explain to Liz that the entire wiring in the house had to be replaced. "One thing after another," he murmured. He made his way back to the crawl space to go and check on Liz and the puppies, but Liz was sticking half way out of it when he approached. Jackson noticed several of his work crew watching her as just her behind continued scooting out of the small space. Seeing their boss, they begrudgingly went back to work instead of staring at the beautiful woman. Holding back his laughter, he waited until she fully emerged before speaking.

"Well, how many?"

She jumped to her feet and almost stumbled over the box behind her, her arms full of momma dog. He grabbed her elbows before she fell and helped her gain her footing. She gently laid the momma dog in the box with her puppies. "Seven puppies," she beamed up at him as she stroked the dog's head. "She did great. I think she is finished."

"Lucky number seven. That's a good amount."

Liz's smile stretched over her face and her blue eyes sparkled. "Mind carrying them inside?"

He reached down as she wiped her dirty hands on her jeans. Jackson's blue t-shirt boasted dirt, blood, and grass stains, and she realized her shirt did not fare any better. "Let's take them through the kitchen." Leading the way, she opened the patio doors. "Mitzy! Grandmother! Come quick!"

Mitzy made it into the room within seconds and her eyes widened at the sight of Liz's appearance. She also stared at Jackson as he navigated his way around the dinette table. Sissy walked into the room and gasped, "Elizabeth, what on Earth happened to you?" She rushed towards her granddaughter before realizing Jackson stood in her home. She noted his appearance and without even looking into the box, turned back to her granddaughter. "Are you two alright? My goodness, is that blood? Are you hurt?" She looked to Liz and then Jackson, both shaking their heads.

"We have puppies!" Liz all but jumped in place as she motioned Jackson to set the box down. He eased the dogs down onto the floor, the momma dog shifting so as to cover and protect her babies. Sissy stood baffled.

"She was under the house. Jackson found her earlier, and poor thing, look how skinny she is. We need to get her food. You know what, I will go to the store. I've got to find my purse." Liz's words were jumbled with excitement as she darted around the room filling a small bowl with water and setting it by the box. She then looked at Jackson and grinned. "I think we have done what most people have tried decades to do."

Confusion had him arching an eyebrow.

"We've made Sissy Montgomery speechless." She giggled as she looked up at her grandmother, their weeks of not speaking melting away as tenderness flooded her grandmother's expression. "It's not everyday my granddaughter and her friend come rushin' into the house covered in blood and mud. Excuse me for catchin' my breath." She placed a hand over her heart as she reached for Liz's hand. Liz threaded her fingers through Sissy's and squeezed. "I should head to the store. Momma there is starving, I'm sure. You can see her ribs."

Liz rushed from the room to go find her purse and Jackson stood, hands in his pockets, as Sissy stared at him. "You can wait outside," she said. Resigned to the fact the woman would never like him, he nodded. "Yes ma'am."

"Oh now, Mrs. Montgomery, let me at least get the boy some lemonade. He looks worn plum out." The old maid clucked around the kitchen.

"Very well, but he will take it on the porch," Sissy ordered. "Though he helped Liz with the puppies, that doesn't change the rules of this house. A Dean waits outside."

Jackson took several steps back and crossed the threshold as Liz emerged back in the room. She watched Mitzy hand him a glass and then saw her grandmother sit at the table. "The dog will sleep in your room, Lizzy. I do not want to have to stumble over puppies and critters."

"Yes ma'am. Jackson could you help me with the box?"

"The boy stays outside," Sissy restated.

"Grandmother," Liz looked up with annoyance. "I thought maybe we were past this. I've had Jackson working inside the house all week up in the east wing."

"But I was not present," Sissy pointed out. "As long as I sit at my table in here, he remains out there."

With finality, she waved her hand in dismissal as Liz stepped outside the doors and shut them behind her with more force than necessary. "And just like that she's back to being an old brute."

Jackson bit back a laugh. "I will admit I was hopeful for a moment, but that quickly faded."

"I am so sorry, Jackson. I don't know what else to say other than that. And I know it doesn't mean much."

"You have nothing to apologize for, Liz. She's her own person."

"I know." She sighed as she began walking towards her car. "I'm going to the store to grab food for the dog." She shouldered her purse. "I should be back in a few."

"Um, when you do—" he trailed off and rubbed a hand over the back of his neck.

"Oh no, what's the matter?" Concern flooded her eyes.

"It's the electrical."

Moaning with annoyance, she closed her eyes a moment. "Let me guess, it has to be replaced?"

He pointed at her as if she answered correctly. "You got it. See the wiring is—"

"You know what," she interrupted. "Just tell me when I get back. I don't want to damper my good mood just yet."

Nodding, he backed up as she slid into her car and shut her door. Rolling the window down, she looked up at him, shielding her eyes with her hand. "Am I causing a standstill by not listening now?"

He shook his head. "Nope, plenty more work to be done. Electrical can wait an hour or so."

"Okay, good. I'll see ya in a bit then. Thanks, Jackson."

He tapped the edge of her window seal as she began backing out of the drive. With a wave, he watched as she turned out onto the road. He then turned back towards the house and saw Sissy standing in an upstairs window watching him. He paused a moment, so that she knew he saw her, and she slowly faded out of view.

∞

Anna sat in Liz's kitchen as Liz continued to marvel over the puppies.

"I can't believe you plan on keeping a dog," Anna laughed as Liz looked at her dumbfounded.

"Of course I'm going to keep her. She obviously has nowhere else to go, and besides, Jackson found her under the house."

"So because Jackson found her you want to keep her?" Anna looked confused.

"No, because she was under *my* house," Liz clarified. She turned as she heard a knock on the patio doors.

"It's the men." Anna announced and waved Ben and Jackson into the house.

Upon entering, Jackson smiled as he squatted down by Liz and rubbed a fingertip over one of the puppy's heads. "They are already looking better." He rubbed a hand over the momma dog's side as she looked at him in adoration. "I see she has a collar now." He fingered the pink, rhinestone encrusted collar around the dog's neck. Her tail thumped as if she expected him to be pleased. "I think it suits you." He rubbed her ears and then grinned at Liz. "Have you named her?"

"Jackson," Liz began formally, "I would like you to meet Lucille."

He continued stroking his hand over the dog. "Lucille it is then. It suits her."

"I thought so too," Liz said proudly.

"Bet you have named all the puppies too," Ben chimed in, looking over the edge of the box before pulling a chair out at the table and sitting next to Anna.

“Maybe.” Liz smiled softly as she stroked each one of the puppies before turning to Jackson. “You here to talk to me about electrical.”

“That was the plan.” He stood, his knees screaming at him for crouching so long.

Standing, Liz made her way to the sink to wash her hands. “I’ll make some lunch while you talk.” She quickly set about removing items from the refrigerator as the other three sat at the table.

“Let’s see, where to start...” Jackson looked to Ben and received no help as Ben sat whispering with Anna and not paying attention. “Well, much like the plumbing, I’m pretty sure the wiring in this house hasn’t been updated since it was installed. Though as we start going through the house, we may find some areas electricians have tied into old wires, but you’re really at the point where you can’t do that anymore.”

“What’s wrong with the old wiring?” Liz asked.

“It’s ancient, for one,” Jackson pointed out. “It’s what’s called knob and tube wiring. Basically you have individual wires: your hot, neutral, and ground, and they come out at a porcelain insulator in the beams and your connections are soldered with cloth tape that’s usually been dipped in tar.”

“Wow, that does sound ancient,” Anna chimed in with a look of regret towards Liz.

"Why would they dip it in tar?" Liz asked curiously.

"Pretty much their way of making electrical tape," Ben explained.

Thoughtfully, Liz nodded. "So what happens now? What do you replace it with?"

"We'll replace it with what's called Romex wiring. This is a three-wire system all encapsulated into one cable. A grouping of the wires, you could say, and they're protected by the tubing," Jackson explained. "But replacing your wiring is not the news I'm worried about telling you."

Liz placed slices of bread on top of the four sandwiches and grabbed a bag of chips off the top of the fridge before handing plates to the group. "Just lay it on me, Jackson."

"To replace this, we are going to have to strip your walls down to the frame."

"All of them?"

"The ones you want to put any outlets on. Most of your rooms only have a single outlet, which was common back then for an overhead light. But if you wish to add more, any wall we have to feed wire through is going to have to be brought down to the skeleton."

Liz looked to Ben as if to test the validity of Jackson's statement. Ben nodded and she sighed as she slipped a chip into her mouth. "This house is going to be the death of me," she murmured.

"Speaking of death," Ben gestured towards Jackson, "show her what you found under the house."

Liz's head popped up. "What?"

Jackson reached into his pocket and pulled out the small shoe. "Found this when I was crawling towards Lucille."

Liz picked up the small boot and turned it over in her hands. "Definitely old and definitely a child's. Was it," she paused to find the words. "Attached to anything?" She already dreaded his answer, but felt a rush of relief when he shook his head.

"If you want, I could look some more and see what else is under there." He offered. "I will admit that my curiosity is piqued."

"I can help you," she said.

"Liz, it is gross under there," Anna protested. "Let Jackson and his men do it. No telling what other creatures are living under there."

"I was under there this morning with Lucille."

"Yeah, but still, how creepy that he found a shoe. There could be bones under there. That would explain some of the ghost theories."

"There are no ghosts." Liz groaned over the subject and rolled her eyes. "You played over here with me as a little girl and did we ever see a ghost?"

"Not that I remember," Anna answered, losing some of her confidence. "But you have to admit the urn flying through the window, the random shoe, the weird noises everyone's been hearing in the walls—"

"What weird noises?" Liz asked.

Jackson shook his head as if he didn't want to have to explain.

"Tell me."

"Some of the men have been a bit weirded out working upstairs due to sounds coming from within the walls."

"Sounds?" Liz prodded. "What kind of sounds?"

Jackson rubbed a hand over the back of his neck before continuing. "A woman weeping."

"I see." Perplexed, Liz slid from her chair and took her plate to the sink. "I don't know anything about a weeping ghost or a weeping woman." She stood with her back to them a minute, collecting her thoughts as she wondered if the weeping woman happened to be her grandmother. There had been several times Liz awoke in the night and heard her grandmother's sobs. She still grieved her grandfather, and the old house, though large, did not muffle sounds of mournful tears. She wondered if her grandmother wept all day. If so, Liz needed to intervene. It hurt her to think of her grandmother in such despair. *No wonder she had been non-existent lately,* Liz thought. *She has a hard time collecting herself.* It had only been six weeks since her grandfather's passing, and over 50 years of marriage and love did not just go away. Sadness did not just disappear overnight. Turning, she found her friends studying her. "Everything okay?" Jackson's kind voice had Liz nodding and forcing a smile. "Of course. Thanks for letting me know. I'll look into the sounds. As far as the electrical, do what you need to do."

"I can show you the plans for upstairs, but as we move downstairs to trace our way to the circuit breaker box, we will have to take out some of these walls as well." He motioned to her kitchen and Liz cringed. "I didn't think of that. Grandmother will have a fit if the downstairs is torn apart."

"I can speak with her," Jackson said, "try and explain the process."

"Right, because coming from you would be *so* much better." Ben laughed and shook his head. "Best let Liz deal with Sissy Montgomery."

"He's right. I'll talk to her." Liz went and sat by the box of puppies as Lucille stood and walked over to her water bowl. The dog's ribs still protruded, but the full food and water bowls told Jackson that it wouldn't be long before the momma dog filled out.

"So what're their names?" Jackson asked, standing over her as he watched her stroke each pup.

Smiling, she pointed to the first one. "This one is Dander, Dan for short," she said, "because if he doesn't get a spot at the breakfast table he gets his dander up."

Chuckling, Jackson knelt down beside the box as well.

"The brown and white one is Bill, after your workman Bill, because he is the one who lent me the flashlight when I went under the house to find Lucille."

"I'm sure he'll be honored," Jackson laughed as he stroked over little Bill.

"And this white little lady is Victoria."

"Formal name," Anna commented from the table as she watched.

"Well, it's because she has a secret."

"Oh really?" Jackson asked.

Liz lifted the solid white puppy to reveal a big brown spot on her belly.

Jackson grinned as she set the puppy back down. "Victoria it is, then."

A throat cleared and had all four friends glancing to the doorway as Mitzy stood there with Sissy behind her. "It's lunch time," Mitzy announced, and in meaning was trying to shoo everyone out of the kitchen so that Sissy could eat in peace.

"I will just take my meal in the parlor, Mitzy," Sissy said, brushing her gaze over Liz and Jackson as they sat beside the puppy box. Without another word, she turned away and the only sound that remained was the echo of her cane walking through the house.

"She is not happy about that boy bein' in the house, Ms. Lizbeth," Mitzy warned with a stern look at Jackson.

Ben and Anna sat awkwardly at the table as Liz met the stern gaze straight on and then turned back to the box. "And these are Belle, Sassy, and Stella. And this little guy is the runt of the litter." She held up a small black puppy and handed it to Jackson. "That one is Dean."

Jackson looked up from the puppy and caught Liz's tender smile as she stroked the small puppy. "He's pretty special," she said. "And I think he is secretly his momma's favorite. I plan on keeping him."

Jackson handed the puppy back to her and she nuzzled her cheek over its little head before laying it gently back in the box as Lucille walked up and accepted the pets and rubs from Jackson and Liz as she made herself comfortable amongst her litter. "All good names," Ben chimed in. "I'll take one when they're ready to leave their momma. It will be nice to have one up at the store."

"Really?" Liz asked. "I definitely think Dander would be perfect for you."

"Why? Because he's a pig?"

She laughed. "No, because he loves a lot of attention. He'll enjoy being the center of attention amongst so many people. Granted they're only a day old, so his personality might change. But I think he would be a good fit."

"Dan the Man is mine then." Ben clapped his hands as he stood. "I've got to head back to the store. As always, fun to see you ladies. Mitzy." He nodded towards the maid as she made a quick sandwich for Sissy. He gestured his head towards outside for Jackson to follow him. Taking the signal, Jackson stood. "Back to work for me as well. I'll let you know what I find." He motioned towards the shoe. Lightly rubbing his finger over Dean the puppy, he followed Ben out.

"You plan on keeping a dog named Dean?" Anna asked. "And you think your grandmother won't have a problem with that?"

Mitzy paused a moment to hear Liz's answer. "Hopefully by the time the puppies are old enough to be given away, Grandmother will love them all and it won't matter."

"You could have named it Jack," Anna suggested.

Liz shook her head. "It means more named Dean."

"And you care that it means something to him?" Anna asked with a slight curve to her lips.

Liz met her friend's gaze and smiled. "Yes. I do."

"Interesting." Anna stroked her chin playfully. "Are you developing feelings for the cute contractor?"

"I didn't say that," Liz corrected. "I simply said that I want him to know that I care about what he did for Lucille."

"Right." Anna stood and shouldered her purse. "How about you leave those puppies for a second and we go get something accomplished at the boutique?"

"It's so hard," Liz said, rubbing her hand over Lucille.

"But necessary." Anna helped pull Liz to her feet and waited at the door as Liz grabbed her purse.

"Tell Grandmother I have news on the electrical work," she told Mitzy. "I would appreciate you letting her know I would like to speak to her at supper tonight."

"Yes ma'am, Ms. Lizbeth. I'll let her know, but I won't make any promises as to her wanting to talk about the house."

Hesitating a moment to decide whether she should go speak to her grandmother right then or to wait, Liz decided work at the boutique needed to be done, and that supper would have to be the time for discussion. Waving at Mitzy and then Lucille, Liz headed out the door with Anna.

«CHAPTER NINE»

Liz took her time. The crumbled newspaper streaked across the window glass as she continued scrubbing to erase the years of grime and dust build up brought by age and disuse. She watched several locals walk by outside on the sidewalk. Friendly waves had her thoughtfully turning towards Anna as her friend scrubbed the baseboards around the room.

“I'm glad I'm back,” Liz announced, causing Anna to pause and look up at her.

“You're just now realizing it?”

“No. Well, sort of,” Liz admitted. “I mean, I guess I've just felt that up until now I was here more for Grandfather and now Grandmother. But being here today, seeing friendly faces outside the window, and working on whipping this place into shape, I just feel like I'm finally here for me too. And I like the idea of being here."

"I certainly love having you back, even though you work me harder than my mother ever did." Anna motioned towards the baseboards as she sprayed the washrag in her hands and continued scrubbing. "Windows are looking better."

"Not quite." Liz blew a defeated breath that caused her bangs to lightly feather up. "I think I need something stronger, chemically speaking, to rub this gunk off. It's sticky, but it will not budge."

Anna looked over and studied the spot on the window. "You should go ask Ben for something. I'm sure he has something that will do the trick."

"Good idea. Mind if I dart up the street?"

Shaking her head, Anna pointed to her purse. "Not if you grab me the largest sweet tea in the tri-county area on your way back."

"Deal." Liz grinned. "My treat though. I'll be back in a few." She grabbed her wallet from her purse before stepping outside, the light breeze a welcome relief after being cooped inside the boutique the last three hours. Walking past the small shops on her street, she took the time to browse. The quaint art gallery boasted paintings of dramatic landscapes, penciled sketches, and pottery. The quilt shop next door displayed an exquisitely crafted double wedding ring quilt that had Liz thinking about the one she had packed away, awaiting her own bed once the remodel was done. The quilt was one of the few belongings she still possessed from her mother. Sighing, she waited patiently at the crosswalk until traffic cleared enough for her to dart across towards the hardware store at the end of the block.

∞

The bell jingled above the door as she entered, and she waved at Ben behind the counter as he wrapped up a conversation with another customer. He flicked a friendly wave as the man turned around, the older gentleman lightly tugging on his hat in greeting to Liz as he exited. She rushed towards the counter and slapped both hands on the countertop. "I am told you can help me, Mr. Wheeler."

"Is that so?" Ben asked, as he crossed his arms over his chest and eyed her with suspicion. "Does it involve baseboard scrubbing? Or remodeling your home?"

"No," Liz assured him.

"Then I am all ears." He grinned as she rolled her eyes and explained the issue of her window residue.

"I've got just the thing, hold on a sec." He disappeared from behind the counter and walked down a nearby aisle. Liz drummed her fingers on the countertop as she waited. The bell above the door sounded and she felt someone step up beside her. She turned her head and smiled in greeting before turning back to look for Ben.

Ben hurried back and slid her a package. "This should work."

He pointed to the older man. "Ah, I will get him for you." Before Liz could pay, Ben darted to the back office area and then quickly came back.

"Okay, let me see..." He typed into the computer and then scanned the package of what Liz now referred to in her head as 'goo remover.'

"$15.95, Liz."

"Geez, for this?" She held it up.

"The price you pay for quality." Ben winked at her as she fished her wallet out of her purse.

"Yeah, yeah, yeah. You're lucky I trust you, Wheeler." She handed him some cash.

Footsteps sounded up the small hallway behind him and Jackson's brows rose. "Hey, Liz."

Glancing up from filing her change into her purse, she smiled. "Hey. Office day?"

Nodding, he glanced to the older man beside her. "Hey, Gramps." He reached across the counter and shook the man's hand.

Jackson noted the surprise in Liz's eyes.

"Gramps, this is Liz Montgomery."

"Ah, the dog rescuer." The older man smiled as he extended a hand. Liz took it cautiously as she eyed Jackson.

"That would be me, though Jackson helped. It is nice to meet you, Mr. Dean. I have heard a lot about you."

"I'm sure you have." He winked conspiratorially and chuckled as she flushed. "You have the look of your mother," he commented. "A beautiful girl and a beautiful heart to match, from what I remember."

"Oh," Liz shouldered her purse. "Thank you. She was... and did, I believe." She flashed Jackson a quick glance before taking the receipt Ben handed her.

"I plan to be out at the house before end of day," Jackson told her.

She waved him away. "Do what you need to do. I wasn't checking up on you or anything. Just needed some goo." She held up her purchase.

"Goo, huh?" Jackson's lips twitched.

"Expensive goo," Liz added dryly as she narrowed a gaze at Ben. He held up his hands innocently as she took a step towards the door. "Well, I should head back. I promised Anna something cold to drink and I have windows to clean." She lingered a moment as her gaze held his. Ronald and Ben's eyes bounced between the two.

"Good luck," Jackson finally added, slipping his hands into his pockets.

With a nod and one last smile at Ronald, she left.

"Pretty little bird," Ronald commented, as he looked at both men before him. "Which of you fellas is goin' to snatch her up?"

Ben held up a hand. "I'm already taken."

"Guess that leaves you, Jack." He laughed. "Honey told me she was coming for the barbeque."

Rolling his eyes, Jackson ran a hand over his jaw. "No, she isn't. Well, not yet. Honey invited her, but Liz isn't sure if she should come due to, well, the whole Montgomery versus Dean issue."

"I sure hope that girl doesn't think we dislike her." Ronald straightened, his crisp button up shirt freshly pressed and pulled taut over his slightly bulging middle.

"It's not so much what you will think," Jackson tried to explain. "I think she is worried what Sissy

Montgomery would think. Her grandmother does not like the fact I'm her contractor, and she barely allows me to enter her home. I don't think she would take too kindly to Liz coming over for a family barbecue. Besides, it's a *family* barbecue. Why would she want to come to that any way?"

"Because we are loads of fun." Ronald tapped his knuckles on the counter.

"Right. How could I forget?" Jackson smirked as his grandfather fished in his pant pockets and wriggled loose change.

"Speaking of fun, how about you join me for a quick break? I need some refreshment. It's hotter than Georgia asphalt out there."

"Sure. Give me a minute." Jackson walked back to his office and Ronald looked to Ben.

"You saw what I saw?" Ronald asked.

"Yep. They've been playing it safe since meeting one another, but there's attraction there. Liz is too devoted to pleasing Sissy to make a move, and Jackson is too respectful of Sissy's outrageous anti-Dean movement to make a move. So here we are." Ben shrugged his shoulders as he stacked several loose papers.

"Shame Sissy has such a hold on the girl. But Sissy always had a strong head on her shoulders, sometimes too strong." Ronald quieted as Jackson emerged.

"Ready?" Jackson walked to the door and held it open as his grandfather slowly made his way over the threshold and pointed. "How about the café?"

"Sounds good." Jackson followed along beside him as they walked to the edge of the street and entered the local hot spot. The café was quiet as only a few people lingered over cool drinks. The after lunch rush had slowed, and the gap between lunch and supper gave a nice atmosphere for an afternoon siesta. Liz turned from the counter with two to-go cups in her hands. She gasped as she almost lost her grip on the cups and slammed into Jackson. "Jackson!" He caught one of the cups and her grip on the second caused the lid to pop off. Thankfully, no liquid was spilt and Jackson's shirt lived to see another day.

"I'm so sorry." Liz reached for the other cup as Jackson steadied her with a small grip to her elbow.

"You alright?"

"Yes, of course. I'm fine. Thanks for saving Anna's drink. Good reflexes."

"No problem." Jackson rocked back and forth on his heels as an awkward silence fell upon them.

"Well, I guess I should go." Liz smiled stiffly as she tried to contain her nerves. "Mr. Dean," she nodded to Jackson's grandfather before hurrying out the door.

Ronald burst into laughter and Jackson eyed him with a curious glower. "Why are you laughing?"

Ronald slapped Jackson on the shoulder. "You've got that poor girl runnin' scared, Jack. What did you do to her?"

"I didn't do anything to her," Jackson defended. "I've just been working on her house."

"You sure that's all you've been workin' on?" Ronald asked, a light twinkle in his eye.

"Yes." Jackson looked confused and had his grandfather laughing again.

"Oh, my boy, Montgomery women can slip past our defenses faster than the Texas Brigade."

Jackson ordered two drinks and then motioned towards a table by the window. He saw Liz walking up the sidewalk towards her boutique and followed her with his gaze until the waitress slid his drink in front of him. "Thank you," he murmured before taking a sip.

"I did love Sissy once." Ronald, nonchalant in his approach to the subject, had Jackson looking at him with concern.

"Oh come now, Jackson. I'm sure you've heard the story by now. You've had to wonder why Sissy does not wish to have you on Montgomery property."

"Yes, Liz explained it to me. I just never thought I would hear you speak of her."

"Why not? History is history. And our individual history shapes us into who we are. Sissy is part of my history, and I hers."

"So what really happened? From her point of view you left her for Honey."

"That is true. Partly."

Jackson looked up the street to verify Liz made it safely to the boutique and saw her enter her building. "What do you mean by partly?"

"George Montgomery was madly in love with Sissy Hanson," Ronald stated.

"But Liz said Sissy didn't really know her grandfather until after she ended things with you. That they met in Florida."

"Pssh." Ronald waved the explanation away. "We all grew up right here in Quinton. Sissy knew George, though not well, mind you, because George was kept on a pretty tight leash. But George and I were friends."

"But you're a Dean and he was a Montgomery. How did you two manage that?"

Ronald chuckled as he shook his head. "Our lands back up to one another, Jack. It wasn't hard. We'd meet out in the woods and play cowboys and Indians. Or better yet Union verses Confederacy. We just never told anyone, especially our families. Even then, the rivalry was strong."

"So what made you give up Sissy for Honey?"

"George had always had a soft spot for Sissy. 'Bout near killed him when she agreed to marry me."

"Why did you ask her then? If you knew George liked her?"

"I didn't. My folks did."

"An arranged marriage?" Jackson asked. "Gramps, even I know that arranged marriages were no longer a thing back then."

"Not an arranged marriage, just something that was encouraged by both parties. We dated and I did love her, but our parents had more of a role in our relationship than we did at times. Poor George was just heartsick over it. We didn't speak for months."

"Why did he not confess his feelings to Sissy?"

"He was too scared." Ronald shook his head at the memory. "George was too kind a friend to disrupt what was already there. My engagement to Sissy had been announced, there was nothing he could do about it then."

"And at what point did Honey enter the scene?" Jackson could just imagine his grandmother in her late teens and the fuss she made when she moved to town. The thought made him smile as he listened closely.

"Let's see," Ronald scratched his chin. "Sissy and I were engaged in June and Honey came in August. So a couple months after the ring. She was the prettiest thing I'd ever seen."

"Sissy or Honey?"

"Your Honey, of course," Ronald scolded. "I knew the first time I saw her that I wanted to marry her. The only problem was, I had Sissy."

"So you continued to fall in love with Honey..." Jackson prodded.

"Yep. Every single day." Ronald's tone sounded whimsical as he continued, and Jackson thanked his lucky stars he came from a family with a history of love and not hate. Or in Liz's case, hurt. "I knew George still had feelings for Sissy, so that's why I didn't feel too badly ending things with her. I knew she and George would be happy together. That he would take care of her and love her in a way I couldn't."

"So they met up in Florida and that's when it all happened for them."

"Yes. George was so excited to have Sissy as his wife. I'll never forget the pleased look on his face when he came back to town. I imagine I looked much the same way with your grandmother. We had our chosen women, and we were happy."

Jackson sipped the last of his drink and slid it to the edge of the table. "I should head back to work."

"Now, hold on a minute, Jack, we are just getting to the good part."

Sighing, Jackson leaned back in his chair and draped his arm over the vacant seat beside him. "Okay, I'm listening."

"Sissy never forgave me for breaking the engagement off."

"As is evident." Jackson pointed a finger at his own chest and Ronald laughed.

"To this day, I still believe she holds a grudge, not because she wanted to marry me, but because she was embarrassed, and felt the entire town was laughing at her. Which wasn't true, but it was the way she felt."

"Liz said her grandparents were very happy together, that they loved one another deeply."

"I imagine they did. George was madly in love with Sissy up until he died. And Sissy loved him, you could tell."

"Then why harbor a grudge towards the Deans? It just doesn't make sense," Jackson countered. "You and George had a chance to end the family rivalry by being friends. Why wouldn't Sissy let it go?"

Ronald shrugged. "I don't know. Not sure if we ever will. The woman has a whole lot of ill feelings towards me locked in that heart of hers. I can't blame her too much, because I did break her heart at the time."

"But like Liz said, that was 50 years ago," Jackson pointed out. "Liz also said that her grandmother is harder now than before George passed away."

"Possibly." Ronald, regretfully, shook his head in dismay. "He was a great man."

Frustrated, Jackson ran a hand through his hair as he leaned forward on both elbows, his hands clasped under his chin. "I don't get it. When I say the woman hates me, I am not exaggerating. She cannot stand to see me in her home and even makes me step across the threshold of the doorway to be outside while she's inside looking right at me." Jackson began telling his grandfather of all his encounters with Sissy Montgomery and when he finished, he leaned back in his seat once more. "And Liz is determined to help Sissy overcome her grief and hatred. Somehow. And she's dedicating all her time into having the house remodeled and repaired because it is what her grandfather wanted for Sissy. Yet, Sissy seems completely opposed to everything. Mostly because I'm a Dean and I'm the one doing the work, but she also will not speak to me on any of the issues. I have to speak to Liz and then Liz conveys the message. Liz thinks she can just love her through it and eventually Sissy will come around."

"Perhaps she can."

Doubtful, Jackson looked at his grandfather.

"It sounds like Liz has the right idea and the right attitude. She also sounds like she just might be stubborn enough to pull it off too. From what you've told me about her, she seems to have the heart and determination for the task."

"I know she does," Jackson agreed. "But I just hate seeing Liz feel defeated when her grandmother treats me rudely. I've offered to hand the work over to another contractor, but Liz won't hear of it."

"That's honorable of you," Ronald complimented. "But have you thought about your role in all this?"

"My role is to fix an old house."

"Maybe. Maybe not. Maybe your presence and your interaction with Liz is what Sissy needs to see. Maybe the fact that you and Liz can be friends will show Sissy that the Deans and Montgomerys can exist without grudges."

"That's Liz's hope."

"But not yours?" Ronald asked.

"Well, yeah, I would love to see Sissy drop her prejudice so that her granddaughter can have a life. But I don't see it happening anytime soon."

"Ah, so you think Sissy is controlling Liz."

"Yes. In a way. Liz is so worried about Sissy or how Sissy is going to react to things that she pushes aside her own wants or needs to make sure she is appeasing her grandmother."

"Pushing aside everything but you," Ronald pointed out. "You said yourself that you've offered to leave and ease the tension between she and her grandmother, but she wants you to stay. Why do you think that is?"

"Because I'm the only contractor who has actually stayed to work on the house."

"And..." Ronald prodded.

Jackson shrugged.

"Because she cares for you," Ronald pointed out.

"What?" Jackson laughed. "Gramps, I don't think you've been listening this entire time. We were discussing Sissy and Liz, not Liz and me. Have we become friends? I would like to think so, or would like to think we are. But the possibility of there being more than friendship is absurd. She's a Montgomery. I'm a Dean. It just wouldn't work."

"Now who's being prejudiced?" Ronald asked with a raised brow. "Think it over, Jack. And think of ways to show Sissy that not all Deans are bad. I'm sure Liz would appreciate the extra help."

«CHAPTER TEN»

Liz sat at the table with her grandmother the next morning sipping her coffee. She was taking it strong and straight as she felt sluggish and sore from yesterday at the boutique. "So he says the walls in here will need to be stripped down in order to replace the wiring and plumbing in here as well," Liz explained. She had been trying to elicit a response from her grandmother for the last twenty minutes, but Sissy just sat, sipping her coffee and filling in her crossword. "I know it's not what we originally planned, but it's necessary, and Grandfather would want me to see this through." *There, that caused at least a small glance up from her paper,* Liz thought.

"Lizzy, your grandfather would be appalled at the state of this house right now." Sissy nudged her glasses back up her nose and went back to the crossword.

“Grandfather asked me to remodel the house. For you. And me. But he wanted you to have a safe and beautiful home to live in. He was upset he wasn’t able to get started on it himself.”

“I do not want to talk about your grandfather.” Sissy’s forced tone told Liz the conversation was over. But she couldn’t help herself.

“Well, I told Jackson to move forward with the plans. He starts down here today. Mitzy said we could use her kitchen while this one is being updated. Jackson said he will make this his top priority so that we can move back into this one as soon as possible.” She stood and walked back to the coffee pot. It was a two-cup kind of morning. She looked outside as several vehicles pulled into the drive. “There they are now.” She reached into the cabinet and pulled out one of her travel mugs and filled it for Jackson. “I’ll be back in a few.”

She met him at the edge of the patio as he and several of his workmen pow-wowed over the day’s tasks. She enjoyed watching him work: confident, knowledgeable, respected. He was kind, but tough, and she realized that that is why his men worked so well for him. Bill gave her a warm smile as he passed and she walked towards Jackson. “Good morning.” He glanced up from his clipboard. She offered him the travel mug.

"If that is coffee, you have saved my life this morning. And quite possibly the lives of my men."

"Busy morning?" she asked.

"You could say that. Thanks for this." He took a long swig and Liz cringed, knowing it had to have burned his tongue, but Jackson never flinched. "Cute." He held up the pink travel mug and she smiled. "I didn't think of the color. Sorry."

"I'm not complaining." He grinned. "So were you able to talk to your grandmother about the kitchen?"

Liz grimaced.

"That bad, huh?"

"Yes. Though I told her we were doing it anyway."

"Look at you, Little Miss Boss."

She laughed. "Hardly. I was wondering though, that while you are in the kitchen, could you move out the dinette table? It's super old, and I thought it might be special to buy Grandmother a new one. A really pretty one to go in her new kitchen."

"Sure. Do you want to donate it?"

"Honestly, it's not really worth donating. I'd just say toss it in the scrap trailer."

"Done. We can do that," Jackson assured her.

"Thanks. I will be up at the boutique today. If you need me for anything, just call." She patted him on the shoulder as she passed, and he turned and watched her climb into her SUV. He answered her wave as she drove away, and he stood a moment thinking how nice it is to see her every morning. He looked at the pink mug in his hand. And it was certainly nice having someone as pretty as Liz bringing him coffee.

"Boss!"

Shaking away the thoughts of Liz, he headed towards the sound of his men.

∞

Liz reached for her phone and noted Jackson's number. Whispering a prayer of thanks, she tossed the metal scraper into the bucket of plaster. "Just the man I needed to speak to. Jackson, I'm afraid I bit off more than I can chew up here at the boutique. I was—"

"Liz, sorry to interrupt, but we have a bit of a situation at the house." He paused, and Liz heard an extremely angry Sissy Montgomery in the background.

"I'm on my way." She looked down at the bucket and sighed. "Oh well," she whispered, as she grabbed her purse and hurried over to the house. What could possibly have her grandmother yelling at Jackson's team? She pulled up to find all of

Jackson's men standing near their vehicles or near their equipment as Jackson stood with his clipboard, arms outstretched as if he were trying to calm her grandmother. Sissy stood on the edge of the patio, her cane thumping in the midst of her tirade. Liz jogged towards the house, several men giving her looks of pity as she approached. "What is going on here?" Breathless, she looked at Jackson, but he was watching her grandmother's cane. She noted the red whelp on his forearm. "Grandmother, *did you hit him*?"

Pointing her cane at Liz, her eyes lashed out before her words. "One step closer, missy, and this cane will find your hide as well."

"You cannot just hit people with your cane! What is going on?"

"That boy has destroyed my kitchen!"

"I told him to," Liz said calmly. "I told you this morning that he would begin work in the kitchen."

"He's taken my table and crushed it! My walls are gone!"

"Grandmother, we talked about this." Liz stepped forward and Sissy raised her cane. Jackson quickly stepped between Liz and Sissy, his eyes sharp and holding a warning.

Sissy pointed her cane at Liz. "You have destroyed my precious home." Her grandmother's voice cracked. "My table..." Her words trailed off as she glanced to the dump trailer. "My table..." She shook her head as tears began to fall. Mitzy rushed outside and eyed them all in surprise.

"Mitzy, would you please take Grandmother to her room? She needs to rest." Mitzy nodded and cupped her hands around Sissy's shoulders as she steered her back towards the house. Sissy turned at the door. "You are not welcome here. Either of you."

Liz watched in shock as her grandmother disappeared through the open doorway. Jackson turned to face her. "I'm sorry, Liz. She just snapped when she came down the stairs and saw the room. The table made her extremely upset."

"I'll go talk to her." Liz nudged passed him and he grabbed her arm before she could enter the house. "I don't know if you should, Liz. Not right now any way. Give her time to breathe."

"No. She hit you." She ran her hand over his arm before stepping back towards the house. "And no matter what state her emotions are in, that is unacceptable. Please, continue your work in the kitchen. I'll be back."

Her shoulders slumped as she stepped into the house. He wished he could walk up the stairs and to the west wing with her to face down Sissy Montgomery, but he knew that would only make matters worse. Whispering a silent prayer for Liz, he whistled for his crewmen to come listen to his plans for the kitchen.

∞

Liz knocked on her grandmother's door and Mitzy slowly opened it to peek out. "I wouldn't, Ms. Lizbeth," she warned softly. Liz shouldered past her and into the room. She marched over to her grandmother with hands on hips as Sissy glanced up from her perch on the sofa. She took a long, measuring sip from her tea as she eyed Liz.

"You had no right to hit Jackson," Liz said, her fury barely in check. "Do you realize what you did?"

"I am well aware of my actions, Elizabeth."

"So you realize that he could press charges? That, technically, you assaulted him? He won't, because he is too kind, but he should. I am appalled at you, Grandmother."

"Now, listen here, Eliz—"

"No, *you* listen!" Liz cut her off with a shout. "You cannot treat people in such a way. Dean or no Dean. Your actions were despicable, embarrassing, and uncalled for. Instead of acting your age, you acted like a ten year old in a tantrum. Jackson was hired to transform our home. Update our home. To turn Grandfather's plans into reality. I am trying to honor those plans. But because of your bigotry and prejudice towards his family, you have attempted to prevent those plans from coming true."

"Are you finished?" Sissy asked.

"Not. Even. Close." Liz fisted her hands on her hips as she stared down at her grandmother. "I have tried, Grandmother. I have tried to be kind to you, to be understanding, but my patience has met its limit. I know you miss Grandfather. I do too. We will miss him forever. And I know you are still grieving, but to lash out at Jackson and his men for doing their job is ridiculous. When I drove up, those men held worry and pity on their faces. Pity! Not for you, Grandmother, but for me. It's disgusting that I should warrant someone's pity because my grandmother is acting like a crazy person! Over a kitchen!"

Sissy took another sip of her tea, the action further infuriating Liz. "This goes much deeper than a kitchen, Grandmother. Much deeper. Now, please, tell me what could possibly warrant you hitting a man you barely know with your cane."

Sissy set her teacup on the coffee table and folded her hands in her lap, ever the dignified lady. Glancing up at Liz, her eyes were clear, no longer damp with tears. "I was distraught." Sissy's simple statement had Liz turning to look and see if Mitzy was witnessing the ridiculous statement and their conversation. Seeing the maid standing behind her, she turned back to her grandmother. "You were distraught? So that's why you attacked Jackson?"

"Oh, calm down, Lizzy, I did not attack him. I simply whacked him for stepping onto the patio after I specifically told him not to. It is my home, I have that right."

"Not when I already gave him permission to be here," Liz pointed out.

"Are you going to let me speak?" Sissy snapped, her calm demeanor slipping a moment as she waved for Liz to sit across from her. "I do not expect you to understand my feelings towards this house, because you and George always had it in your heads to change it."

"Grandfather said that—" Her grandmother's stern stare had her defense halting.

"I've always enjoyed the home how it is. It has been my home for over 50 years, and it has served me well. It doesn't need a fancy new kitchen or new walls, it is fine the way it is. And my table—" she paused a moment as her voice cracked. "That table was a gift from your grandfather for our 25th wedding anniversary. We sat there every morning together. We ate there, prayed there, laughed there, shed tears there. That table is where we sat to work the crosswords, discuss our daily to-do lists, to discuss you and your life. It held memories. And you and that Dean boy just tossed it into the dump without a thought."

"I-I didn't know," Liz admitted. "You never told me that story."

"You never asked." Sissy stood and made her way to the large window overlooking the front yard and drive. Jackson's men continued working on the exterior of the house despite the showdown earlier. Liz appreciated Jackson's dedication and was continually impressed with his crew. "You may finish the east wing renovations," Sissy continued. "Your grandfather would want you to have a place of your own, and with the changes being made, you will. I wish to have the downstairs kitchen complete by Monday."

"It's Friday, Grandmother. Jackson's crew will not be working through the weekend."

"It will be completed by Monday, or you will need to find a new place of your own."

"*You're kicking me out*?" Liz's voice rose in surprise. "Of my own home?"

"It is not your home yet, and until it is, you will do as I say."

"But your deadline is unrealistic. They could possibly have it completed by next Friday at the earliest."

"The deadline is Monday, or you move. I will not speak of this again."

"Is this why you've been doing all the silly ghostly acts? To scare away any contractor that might work on the house? Because you do not want changes to be made?"

"I do not know what you mean."

"The urn through the window? The weeping in the walls?" Liz asked.

Perplexed, Sissy looked at Liz. "Weeping? I have not been weeping in the walls. That is absurd."

"Well, several of the men have reported hearing it. And they certainly didn't make up the urn flying through the window. Jackson and I were there."

"I would not destroy my home to make a point. That seems to be more your style. Now go, I'm sure you need to tell Mr. Dean of his new deadline." Sissy turned back towards the window and ignored Liz as she slowly made her way to the door with heavy steps.

When she reached the stairs, Liz hurried down and stepped outside the front door. Shock and disbelief had her slamming the door. She needed to gather herself before she told Jackson the impossible deadline. Her breathing grew uneven, a heavy weight pressed down on her chest, and she felt the tears burning behind her eyes as her back slid down the door until she sat.

She circled her arms around her knees, bent her head, and cried.

∞

That's how he found her. Jackson heard the door slam and knew it had to be Liz. After the encounter with Sissy, he knew the two women would exchange words. But what he was not ready for was the sight of Liz sobbing, her shoulders shaking as she hid her face in her knees. Every thought in his head told him to turn around and give her space, but his heart seemed to move his feet forward. He reached the bottom step before her head popped up. Her cheeks stained with tears, her mascara smudged beneath her eyes. She looked… bereft. Lost. *And completely beautiful,* he realized. She cleared her throat and quickly grabbed the bottom hem of her t-shirt and attempted to wipe her eyes. "Jackson—" her voice laden with tears had him moving forward and kneeling before her. He lifted her chin with his hand and studied her a moment. "Tell me about it."

Her lips quivered as she mustered another breath and another tear escaped. He continued his way down and moved from kneeling to sitting beside her. He draped an arm around her shoulders and felt her shudder as another swarm of sobs took hold of her. She turned her face into his shoulder as she cried. And he let her. After witnessing Sissy Montgomery in action, he could only imagine how Liz must be feeling. And at the moment he wondered how Liz could even live with such a woman. He did not understand Liz's love for her grandmother, especially when the lady could have such a strong woman like Liz crying on the porch.

"Sh-she wants the kitchen com-pleted b-by Monday," Liz stuttered.

He gently rubbed her shoulder as she sniffled, rather unglamorously, and then hiccupped.

"B-by Monday, or... or I h-have to m-move out."

Her last words had Jackson's body tensing. How could Sissy force such an ultimatum upon Liz? She had no control over how fast his crew moved. Nor did she have control over all the potential problems or hazards that awaited them with such a deadline. He stopped his own thoughts a moment to realize Liz had calmed and her sobs were now just soft sniffles. She looked up at him, her eyes burdened by grief. He lightly brushed his fingers over her face as he tucked her hair behind her ear. "Monday it is, then."

A sob escaped her lips as she forced a smile. "It's okay, Jackson." She eased away from him as she swiped her eyes once more and leaned her head back against the door and sighed.

"I'll go talk to the men and see who would be willing to work late and through the weekend. We can get it done." He started to rise, but Liz placed a hand on his arm. Pausing, he looked at her.

"It's okay. I know it's a ridiculous deadline. Her goal is for the house not to be changed, and if she would prefer to live in it as is and without me, so be it."

"Liz, this is your home too. No matter what she said. And I'm sure once she considers her words, she will regret them and wish for you to stay."

"We are talking about Sissy Montgomery, right?" Liz sneered. "The woman who can hold a grudge for 50 years?"

"There is that." Jackson rubbed a hand over his jeans as he flexed his fingers.

"Besides, it wasn't the kitchen being destroyed as much as it was the table. The table is what set her off. I didn't realize how special it was to her." Liz blew a shaky breath. "You know, I started this whole project to make her feel Grandfather's love, and my love, even more, and all I've done is cause her more heartache. And for that, I am frustrated and disappointed with myself. How could I not see how she felt?"

"Because of me," Jackson added.

"What?"

"She wasn't speaking to you, because of me being here. Your choice to hire me resulted in her not speaking to you. She probably would have been more open about her feelings had they not been hurt by my presence."

"You're probably right," Liz agreed and lightly gripped his arm in a reassuring squeeze. "Though I still stand by my decision of hiring you and do not regret that decision." She offered him a supportive smile.

"Well, how can we change her mind? Blow her away with her new kitchen?" he asked.

Shrugging, Liz rose to her feet and then offered a hand to Jackson. Rising, he ran his thumb over her knuckles before releasing her hand. *How had he become so comfortable with Liz? When did it happen?* He purposely took a step back, unwilling to admit he'd become emotionally involved with the pretty brunette, but he felt drawn to her. *Had been since the first day he saw her,* he reminded himself. But something was different between them now. Perhaps it was the whacking from Sissy that woke him up. Either way, he cared for Liz. And if working all night and through the weekend was to save her from having to move out of her family home, he would do it.

"I'm going to tell the men. You going to be okay?"

She nodded. "Thanks for… well, everything. And I'm so sorry Grandmother hit you with her cane. I cannot even begin to describe how sorry I am for that."

He waved her apology away. "Only stung for a second." Winking, he walked down the porch steps. "I'll let you know the game plan as soon as we come up with one."

A game plan was already circling around in his head, and though he would have to miss the family barbecue later in the evening, he felt his grandparents would understand. He reached into his pocket and pulled out his phone.

"Gramps, hey, it's Jackson." Pausing, he listened to the familiar greeting his grandfather bestowed upon him since he was five years old. "Hey there, Jack Boy! How's it hangin'?"

"Not so good actually. I, uh, won't be able to make it to the barbecue tonight. Something has come up here at the Montgomery house and I'm needing to finish a project."

"And you're leaving it to me to tell Honey? You are no longer my favorite grandson."

"I was your favorite? Since when?" Jackson grinned as his grandfather took a dramatic pause.

"Well, since last week, of course."

"Ah, last week, right." Jackson chuckled. "Well, I hate to ruin that streak I had going, but yeah, I'm up against a steep deadline. Send my apologies to Honey."

"I will, I will. Is there anything else you needed?"

Jackson's gaze swept over the dump trailer. The small dinette table and chairs were piled amongst scraps of wood, several of the chairs with broken legs or supports. An idea sparked. "Actually, Gramps, I have a favor to ask."

∞

"Thank you, thank you, thank you! Liz hugged Anna before helping her friend unload grocery bags from the backseat of her beetle. "You are a lifesaver."

"I am still in shock over what you said over the phone. Your grandmother is seriously threatening to kick you out?"

"Yep."

"Wow. I'm sorry, Liz."

"It's okay. Jackson is determined to complete the kitchen by Monday. If it doesn't happen, it was not for lack of trying. So thank you, for picking up groceries for me. I'm going to feed these men since they are giving up their weekend to help me."

"They are getting paid already, Liz," Anna reminded her.

"Yes, but they have all been working with such urgency and determination, and that, I know, is because they are wanting to genuinely help me."

“So where do you plan on cooking this? Considering the only other kitchen is in Mitzy’s quarters?”

“That is a good question.” Liz hadn’t thought that one through and she inwardly kicked herself. Faced with a dilemma, her head spun even more when she saw Ginger Dean’s car roll up the drive. “Oh, what does she want?” Liz murmured. “That woman honestly tries my patience. It’s like she’s asking for a fight with Grandmother.”

“Maybe she is here to see why Jackson isn’t at the barbecue.”

“He already told his grandfather he wasn’t going to make it,” Liz pointed out and plastered on a smile as Ginger Dean swung her legs out of her car, her spikey heels landing deep into the dirt as she stood. “Hello, girls!” She waved and adjusted the silk scarf covering her hair before walking towards them. “I have an entire trunk full of food for Jackson and his boys. Would you ladies mind helpin’ me unload?”

“Food?” Liz asked.

“Why yes, we can’t let them go hungry. Not when they are workin’ on the double.” She winked at Liz and eyed the grocery sacks in her hands. “Seems we had the same idea, sugar bean.” She patted Liz’s arm before turning back towards her car. “Come on now, I’ve only got two hands.”

Liz and Anna stuffed the bags back into Anna's car and followed Ginger. The woman pulled two large foil pans from the trunk and handed one to Anna and one to Liz. She then stacked loaves of bread on top of them. "I'll get the potato salad. You girls go set that up. I'll follow."

Liz started walking towards the house and then paused, turning back towards Jackson's grandmother. "Mrs. Dean—"

"It's Honey or Ginger, darlin', and no, there is no need to thank me. I am just feedin' my grandson, after all." She winked again and walked towards the house. Without stepping foot on the patio, Ginger called for Jackson. He poked his head out the door and immediately rushed out. "Honey, what are you *doing* here?"

"I've brought food. Turn one of those boards into a table, won't you, Jack? The girls and I will set up." Jackson stood dumbfounded as he watched Anna and Liz walk up. "Chop, chop, sweetheart, you don't want the food to get cold."

Jackson quickly set up two sawhorses and placed a large piece of plywood on top of them. Ginger set down the potato salad and then walked back to her car as Liz slid one pan onto the wood.

"Liz, I didn't know." Jackson, an apology on the tip of his tongue stopped as Liz released a relieved smile. "I'm actually completely fine with this, Jackson. I'm grateful."

Ginger walked back up lugging a large cooler. Anna quickly intercepted and scooted it near the table.

"There's barbecue, potato salad, bread, sauce, and drinks. I saw you girls had some cookies in those grocery bags, so I will say you can cover dessert." She hugged Jackson and kissed his cheek. Then held her arms out to Liz. Awkwardly, Liz stepped forward and Ginger swept her into a bone-crushing hug with a light rub on her back. "You hang in there, sweetie. Sometimes us old ladies take a while ownin' up to our foolishness. Sissy is no different. She'll come around, just you wait and see." Releasing Liz, Ginger jingled her keys. "I'd best get back to the barbecue. Jackson, your father refused to come… again." She cast him a dissatisfied glare. "Be sure to tell him we are disappointed he has not overcome that ill-placed pride of his next time you speak to him."

"Yes ma'am. Thanks, Honey." He watched as his grandmother hurried away, her trail blazing speed spewing up gravel as she went. He looked to Liz. "I'll rotate men out for breaks that way the work doesn't come to a complete standstill."

"Okay." Liz held his gaze a moment, his dark eyes kind and understanding. She noted the small trace of weariness and immediately felt guilty for being the reason it was there. Anna nudged her and Liz realized the moment to move on had long since passed and she and Jackson still stood eyeing one another. Whatever this was, this... attraction... friendship... feeling... she didn't know, but she felt the tug in her heart when she looked at him. "Thanks."

"Thank me when it's done. You ladies go home to Anna's and get some rest. We'll see you in the morning." He darted a glance towards Anna as if to commission her in pulling Liz away. Without fail, Anna did so, and she made it a point to keep conversation to a minimum on their way to her house, knowing full well Liz's mind was elsewhere.

«CHAPTER ELEVEN»

"You're up early," Anna yawned as she shuffled her way towards the coffee pot, her pink fuzzy slippers dragging against the tile.

"I wanted to get a head start on making the sandwiches for the crew." Liz motioned towards a pile of foil wrapped sandwiches stacked on the edge of the counter.

"You realize it is only 7:30, right?" Anna asked, sliding onto a bar stool and watching her friend smear mayonnaise on wheat bread.

"Yes, but I figure we can put these in a cooler for the guys to eat later, while we head over there in about 15 minutes or so."

"You want me to be ready in 15 minutes?" Anna rested her chin in her hand and stifled another yawn. "I don't know if I'm going to make that deadline."

"I promise to stop for coffee *and* donuts on the way."

Anna slid to her feet. "Done. I'll just dry shampoo this hot mess called my hair and save time not showering."

"Gross," Liz teased, as she began wrapping another sandwich. She then stacked all the sandwiches into a small cooler and placed freezer packs on top before closing the lid. "That ought to do it," she muttered, testing the cooler's weight as she reached for the two grocery bags containing bags of potato chips. She couldn't wait to swing by the house and see how much work Jackson and his crew had accomplished. She knew they must be exhausted, and she wasn't quite sure how she could ever repay Jackson for the extra effort.

True to her word, Anna bounced back into the kitchen with her hair tied up into a messy bun and her mascara wand in her hand. She paused at the mirror above the entry table and swiped mascara over her lashes. "I'm ready when you are."

Liz grabbed the food and followed Anna out the front door.

"Think they were able to get the walls up last night?"

"I hope so." Liz shut the car door and buckled her seat belt as Anna did the same. "Though I know there was still some electrical work that had to be completed." Liz wound her hands in her lap and began popping her knuckles.

"Stop that," Anna scolded.

"What?" Liz looked over confused.

"You're popping your knuckles, and you only do that when you are nervous or worried. Trust me when I tell you that you have nothing to be worried about. Jackson is not going to let your grandmother kick you out. He cares about you too much."

"I know, but— wait, what did you say?" Liz asked.

"I said, he cares for you," Anna repeated and noted her friend's lack of acknowledgment. "Oh come on Liz, please tell me you've noticed."

"What? No. Why would I? He is just my contractor."

"Seriously?" Anna laughed. "I had to all but pull you away from him yesterday afternoon. Y'all were all but makin' out on the patio."

Liz's face flushed at the accusation. "We were no such thing! He was telling me his plan for the evening work."

"Oh, well, I guess that's what it was then." Anna giggled as Liz slapped her arm. "I guess I must have imagined it during the ten minutes you two made googly eyes at one another."

"Oh my goodness, Annie, stop it!" Liz placed her hands over her warm cheeks but could not help the laugh that bubbled up out of her chest. When Anna pulled into the parking lot of the donut shop, Liz hopped out.

"Extra sprinkles!" Anna called after her as Liz shut the door. She acknowledged the request with a flick of her hand as she darted inside. Less than five minutes later, Liz hurried back to the car. "Okay, so maybe I have started to have some feelings for him," Liz admitted.

Anna's brows rose. "Oh, are we still talkin' 'bout Jackson?" She grinned as Liz shrugged.

"Well, I figured you would keep pestering me about it, so I might as well admit what I'm feeling."

"I would definitely say those feelings are mutual," Anna added. "He can't take his eyes off of you, he's going out of his way to make your dreams come true with the house and this ridiculous deadline, and he seems to truly care about helping you mend things with Sissy."

“Exactly,” Liz agreed. “I mean, he does seem committed to more than just remodeling the house. But then I worry about whether or not I’m reading too much into it. I mean, he is a nice guy, and nice guys do nice things. Maybe he’s just being…”

“Nice,” Anna finished with a smirk.

Liz pointed at her as if she answered correctly. “Right.”

“Well, I think it’s more than niceness that has him staring at you.” Anna mimicked an open mouth gape and Liz laughed.

“Stop it, he does not look at me like that.” Though Liz secretly wished he did. “Besides, it could never happen.”

“You still beatin’ that ol’ horse to death?” Anna asked.

“What old horse?” Liz asked.

“The ‘he’s a Dean and I’m a Montgomery’ horse.” Anna rolled her eyes as she pulled into the drive of the Montgomery house. “Well, it’s still standing. Guess Sissy didn’t smoke ‘em out.”

“You are just on a roll this morning, aren’t you?” Liz slid out of the car and leaned on her door to survey the house.

"It's what happens when you wake me up before 9 AM while I'm on summer vacation." Anna shut her door and waited for Liz to round the hood before walking towards the house with donuts.

Liz noticed Bill asleep in one of the work trucks, his cheek smushed up against the passenger window as several workmen hurried around the worksite. The sounds of hammering echoed in the morning breeze as Liz stepped over the threshold and into the kitchen. She gasped as her eyes traveled over the newly installed walls. Jackson stood on a ladder plastering the ceiling. He looked down as she stared up at him. "You guys have been busy." She smiled as he climbed down and rested his hands on his hips.

"You could say that. We've had shifts going most of the night." He motioned for them to step outside to avoid standing in the way.

"Wow, that breeze feels nice," he commented as he eyed the boxes in Anna's hands. "Are those donuts?"

She opened the lid and he took two without hesitation and stuffed half of one in his mouth. "Sorry, I'm starving."

Liz handed him her coffee and he took a long sip. "Wow, I think this will kick me into gear. Not going to lie, I'm starting to lag."

"Did you take a break at all?" Liz asked, already knowing the answer.

"Not yet." Jackson pointed to the truck where Bill slept. "I'm after Bill... potentially."

Liz gently rubbed a hand over his back as he stood next to her facing the house. "You need rest too," she commented.

"I'll get some." Avoiding the topic, he pointed to a man standing over rows of crown molding. "Pete will be installing the molding this afternoon. Electrical and plumbing were completed around midnight. Insulation went in on the exterior wall and then the sheetrock. We are working on plastering everything. I figured you would want it to look as much like it did as possible, plus keeping with the integrity of the house, we are trying to keep it historically accurate."

"Yes," Liz nodded as she watched the transformation. "I can't believe you have accomplished so much in one night."

Jackson took a bite of his donut as Lucille wandered up to Liz, her tail wagging. "Hey little momma," Liz stroked the dog's head. "Did you have a noisy night? How are our babies, hmm?"

"I checked on them around three or so." Jackson patted Lucille as she jumped up, resting her paws on his thigh. "Gave her fresh food and water. I wasn't sure if you remembered to before you left."

"I completely forgot. Thanks for doing that. Poor girl, I'm sorry." Liz smiled as Lucille accepted the apologetic rubs. "Well, Anna and I brought donuts for breakfast and then we have a cooler full of sandwiches for lunch. I'll put them on your truck bed and the men can grab whatever, whenever."

"You don't have to feed us, Liz."

"Yes, I do." She turned her face to the sun as it slid up over the house and lit the east wing. She saw a curtain shift in an upstairs window. Either Mitzy or her grandmother watched. She started to step forward, but Anna grabbed her arm. "I wouldn't."

"Why?"

"I would let her see the deadline be met and then you can go talk to her."

"She would think me gloating," Liz pointed out with an edge of glum. "I should go speak with her and see if her mind has changed. Perhaps after sleeping on it, she has had a change of heart. Especially since she's probably heard the work all night."

Jackson reached for her the second time she attempted to enter the house. "There's something else you should know, Liz."

"I'm listening." Cautiously, she looked up at him and saw the dread within the tiredness.

“Last night, the crew and I heard a woman weeping again. And I know it was not coming from your grandmother’s wing of the house. It felt as if it were right behind us, above us, around us... I can’t really explain it. But it was definitely sobbing. I had two men leave because of it. Superstition got the better of them.”

“Hmm.” Tapping her fingers against her chin, she turned to Anna. “Want to explore some of the secret passage ways this morning?”

“Are you kidding? Not when there’s a woman hidin’ in them.” Anna shuddered. “What if we find her?”

“Then I would love to know why she’s in my house.” Liz laughed at Anna’s nerves. “Trust me, there’s no one in the walls. You say the sound moved?”

“Pretty much anywhere we went, it sounded,” Jackson explained. “Also, the power was disconnected twice. Just a breaker or two, but always in the area we were working. Easy fix, but it wasn’t being thrown by too many pieces of equipment running. Someone manually flipped the breakers.”

“It would seem there’s a bit of sabotage going around. I’ll look into it.” Liz motioned for Anna to follow, but her friend shook her head. “No thanks. I choose to live.”

Shaking her head on a laugh, Liz walked into the kitchen.

"I'm coming with you," Jackson said, his hand at the small of her back as she led the way to the front parlor.

"There's an entrance into the wall in here." She nudged a wall panel and it gave way to a sliding door. She stepped inside and to the right, Jackson following close behind her. "You have a flashlight?"

He pulled one out of his tool belt. "Ready and waiting." He handed it to her as she flicked it on. "This wall backs up to the kitchen; I'm sure you noticed."

"Yes. We didn't have to bust into the old walls. It seems there's a gap between the spaces. Each passage is sandwiched between two walls. So we never tore into the actual passages, because they are separated off from the main walls."

"Interesting. I didn't realize that," Liz commented, as her light flicked over the path before them. They passed a bench here and there, boxes of memorabilia, old newspapers. The passages served as extra attic space and had for years. The history contained in the presence of the passages themselves was nothing compared to the history littering its floors.

"Have you been able to crawl under the house again?" Liz asked, as she shined the light up ahead.

Jackson swatted away a spider web as he followed. “No, not yet, but I want to. I’ll get to it eventually.”

“Don’t stress about it, Jackson. It’s not on the contracting list.” She looked over her shoulder and smiled. “Besides, you are already going above and beyond.” She paused as she heard an echo of footsteps. “Did you hear that?” she whispered. “Someone’s in the passageways.”

Jackson reached for the flashlight and stepped in front of her to take the lead, and Liz did not put up a fight as she clasped the back of his shirt in her hand to hold onto him.

“How many people know of the passages?” Jackson whispered.

“Just Grandmother, Mitzy, and me. Well, and my grandfather knew.”

He stopped and Liz bumped into him with a small grunt. “Sorry,” she whispered, her words close to his ear.

“I don’t hear it anymore.” He turned left and followed the beam of light, his gaze flashing ever so often to what sat stacked along the walls. “What’s in all these crates and boxes?”

“Your guess is as good as mine. Grandfather and I had planned on sifting through everything this fall as the temperatures grew cooler, but…” Her voice trailed off as she reached around him and gripped his wrist, moving the light to a short stool. "Look at that."

Jackson stepped forward and reached down and picked up a small compact disc player. He pressed play and the sounds of a woman's sobs echoed down the hollow space. He stopped it. "Guess we found our ghost."

Liz grabbed the device and opened it, the disc blank. "Who would do such a thing?" Her eyes darkened. "She's trying to scare away the crew." Shaking her head, she slammed the player back down on the stool. "I cannot believe she would sink so low."

Jackson held up his hand, "Come on now, Liz. Innocent until proven guilty."

She shot him a look that could kill, and he grinned. "You can fire those flaming darts at me all you want, but we both know your grandmother isn't the only one walking the passages. You said Mitzy knows of them as well. Could it be she is doing it?"

"Mitzy? No. Why would she? She has no reason." Liz ran a hand through her hair, the soft waves beckoning Jackson's fingers. He clinched his fist to prevent reaching out.

"You know what? Forget it. Grandmother obviously doesn't want me to live here. I might as well give her what she wants."

"Hey," Jackson lifted her chin. "It is not that your grandmother doesn't want you here, Liz. She just doesn't want the house to change."

"It still angers me," she admitted, her eyes becoming glassy.

"Come on now, don't do that to me again." He rubbed his thumb over her cheek and she looked away before any tears fell. She shook her head and held the heels of her hands to her eyes. "I'm not, I'm fine." Though her voice wasn't as strong as it had been earlier, her self-control fell back into place. "Let's get out of here." With a last dejected look at the disc player, Liz turned back the way they had come, leaving Jackson in the dark.

∞

"You would think after all we've been through the last couple of months she would just talk to me." Liz grunted as she carried her end of the heavy oak table across the room. Anna shuffled her feet as she lifted the other end. "To place a CD player in the passage ways? How childish!"

They set the table beneath the window and both heaved sighs of relief. Liz dusted her hands on her jeans before walking back to the storage room to retrieve a tall cabinet. Anna followed.

"Maybe it's like Jackson said and it's just Mitzy playing tricks. That woman has always given me the willies."

"What?" Liz asked. "Mitzy scares you? How come I never knew this? And why?" She ended on a bewildered laugh.

"Because she was always around with her eagle eyes." Anna widened her eyes for affect as she leaned disapprovingly over Liz. Laughing, Liz shoved her away. "Seriously, the woman was just scary, and even as a grown up, I still find her odd."

"Mitzy has a good heart," Liz defended. "She has also earned her weight in gold the last month since Grandfather died. She's been there for Grandmother in ways I can't be, especially right now since I'm not allowed to stay there."

"But you will be. Once Jackson is done with the kitchen."

Shrugging, Liz looked at the wall she had started to texturize several days ago. The uneven drywall mud appeared unfinished and sloppy, since she was pulled away mid-project the day her grandmother lashed out at Jackson. She grabbed a washcloth and swiped it over the cabinet she wished to move.

"I say we take a break," Anna interrupted, eying the cabinet with trepidation. "Let's go to the café and grab some lunch, then we can come back and I might be up for moving that beast." Nodding towards the cabinet, Anna walked towards the door. "You're buying, by the way."

Grinning, Liz tossed the washcloth into a bucket of soapy water. "It's the least I can do. Plus, I need to call Jackson and see how the kitchen is coming. I haven't heard from him today, and I've left him two messages."

"He's busy, Liz."

"He could at least text me an update."

"Are you sure you are wanting to know about the kitchen, or are you just wanting an excuse to talk to Jackson?" Anna waited as Liz locked the door to the boutique then linked her arm through Liz's. "Well?"

"Well, what?" Liz asked, causing Anna to jerk her arm slightly. "Answer my question."

Sighing, Liz avoided Anna's direct gaze so as not to embarrass herself further. "Maybe it's a little of both. Don't gloat." She pointed a finger at Anna before her friend could respond.

"I won't gloat," Anna promised. "I will just give a dramatic, 'I see.... Do tell, Elizabeth.'"

Liz opened the door to the café and they stepped in line to wait their turn to order. "I think I may be starting to have fe—"

“Heavens to Betsy! Why, it’s Liz Montgomery in the flesh.” A shrill voice drew the women’s attention to the line ahead of them and Liz’s stomach dropped to her toes.

“Lilly Barker, is that you?” she asked in the most polite voice she could muster.

“It’s Lilly Andrews now,” Lilly sneered and her eyes browsed over Liz like a wolf circling its prey. “I had heard you were back in town. I’m surprised. I figured you would never return to Quinton. Why, with your big city plans and all.”

“Well, my family is here,” Liz pointed out, trying to keep the edge from her voice.

“Yes, of course. Speakin’ of,” Lilly continued, her smile widening. “I heard you and your grandmomma weren’t on speakin’ terms.” She feigned an apologetic face. “I sure hope it doesn’t have anything to do with your relationship with that new contractor.”

Liz’s brow lifted. “I’m sorry?”

“Well, Jackson Dean, of course. I hear he is quite the looker. But I can see how your grandmomma would have a problem with him, him bein’ a Dean and all.”

“I really don’t think that is any of your business,” Anna added, earning a wicked grin from Lilly.

"Honey, this is Quinton. Everything is everyone's business. Especially when it involves the Deans and the Montgomerys."

"Well there is no relationship between Jackson and me, so unfortunately I do not have any new information for you." Liz stepped forward to nudge Lilly towards the counter. The bell above the door rang as others entered the café, and Lilly's attention diverted long enough for her to muster an evil chuckle. "Why, if it's not the man of the hour right now." She winked at Liz.

Liz turned around and Ginger Dean waved with her arms outstretched as Jackson continued holding the door for other patrons. "Oh, Elizabeth!" Ginger hugged her affectionately. "How are you doin', sweetheart?" She rubbed Liz's arms before squeezing her hands. "Jack, look who it is." Smiling proudly, Ginger turned to her grandson. Jackson's eyes met Liz's and he smiled. "Hey Liz," he nodded towards Anna, "Anna."

"Hey."

Lilly stepped forward and extended her hand. "Lilly Andrews."

Jackson shook her hand, but before he could speak, Lilly had shouldered her way next to him and linked her arm with his. "Liz was just tellin' me that you were workin' on her family home. I dare say that must be an enormous undertakin'."

Jackson started to respond, but Lilly continued. "Liz and I went to high school together. We go way back."

Liz and Anna attempted to hide their distaste, but Ginger's brows lifted at the interaction.

"See, Liz used to have this enormous crush on my husband. Though back then we were just datin'. Liz had hoped Marcus would take her to prom, but instead he asked me." She giggled with a hand over her heart. "We've been inseparable ever since." She held out her hand with the sparkly diamond ring on her ring finger.

Jackson wasn't quite sure what to say, so he looked to Liz for rescue. She just shrugged her shoulders with an apologetic tilt to her lips.

"I am so glad we ran into you two ladies." Ginger grabbed Liz and Anna's shoulders and turned them towards the counter and left Jackson to fend for himself. "I was thinkin' that I could help with supper again tonight for the crew. Now, I have some ingredients for some casseroles, but I could really use help with the assembly. You girls wanna come by the house about four? We could whip them together and have them out to the Montgomery house by six."

"Oh, Mrs. Dean—" Liz started to interject, but Ginger cut her off. "It's Ginger, dear, how many times must I tell you? And don't go givin' me an excuse about not steppin' foot in the Dean home. At this point, we should all be past that little kerfuffle." They both turned as Lilly released a shrill giggle. Jackson's eyes flashed desperately for freedom and Liz bit back a smile. "Excuse me," she stepped away from Ginger and Anna and walked up to Jackson and slid her arm through his. "Lilly, if you would excuse us, Jackson and I have much to discuss."

Lilly eyed her suspiciously as she unlinked herself from Jackson. "Well, I need to meet up with my group anyhow." She stepped away from Jackson but lingered as if thinking of one last word to say to Liz.

"I'm glad you were able to take a break today and join us for lunch." Liz looked up at Jackson adoringly and he tapped her chin with his finger. "I wouldn't have missed it."

Lilly turned in a huff and walked away.

"I apologize in advance for whatever she told you about me," Liz muttered under her breath as they stepped forward.

"Oh, she was just regaling me with stories from the 'good ol' days.' Her words, not mine." He winked at her as she shook her head.

"Most probably exaggerated or untrue," Liz explained.

"I picked up on that myself." Jackson waved her ahead of him so she could order and caught the pleased expression on his grandmother's face. *If only there was something brewing between he and Liz for her to be pleased about,* he thought. Then again, he did sense a change in Liz towards him, especially after her crying episode on the porch. He hoped so anyways. Because he found he spent too much time thinking of her throughout the day, and not in a professional sense.

"We'll go fetch a table," Anna hollered as she and Liz walked away.

Ginger rubbed a small circle on his back as he ordered and they patiently waited as the host filled their drinks. "I find her absolutely charming," Ginger whispered. "And stunning. Why, Jack, I think you and Elizabeth would make a handsome pair."

"Honey..." he warned softly. "Don't go there."

She held up a hand in innocence. "I'm your grandmomma, sugar. I'm supposed to go there. I want the best for you. And that girl is as pretty as a peach on a hot summer's day and sweet as all get out. If you don't line yourself up in the front of the line, it won't be long and she will have multiple men vyin' for her attention."

"Honey—"

"I mean it, Jackson. Look at her." Ginger watched as Jackson flicked a gaze in Liz's direction and she happened to look towards them. Their eyes met and she immediately smiled, a warm blush staining her cheeks before she turned back to Anna.

"Ah, now see, that girl has a pull on her heart for you too." Ginger reached for her drink as she hurried towards the other two women. Jackson followed, rubbing a hand over the back of his neck before glancing at his watch.

"You can take time for lunch, Jackson." Liz grinned as he slid into the booth seat next to her. "In fact, I bet this is the first break you've actually taken since taking on the deadline."

"I've taken breaks." His words died off as she peered at him with disbelief. "Well, I've taken a few minutes here and there."

"Right," Liz continued. "Again, I'm super grateful, but you also look exhausted. When was the last time you slept?"

Not remembering, he stayed quiet as their food was served.

"Exactly. I don't want you working yourself to death. If the deadline is not met, I can stay with Anna until I figure something else out."

"No." Jackson's abrupt dismissal left her surprised. "The deadline will be met."

"Jackson—"

"No, Liz. It will be met. End of discussion. And don't worry about me. I'm fine. The crew is working hard as we speak. I had to run to town to pick up a few things from Ben, and Honey nabbed me, otherwise I'd be back there already. But Bill assures me things are still running along fine."

"I'm sure they are." Liz watched as he glanced at his watch again before taking a hearty bite of his sandwich.

"I just don't want you overdoing it on my behalf," Liz softly whispered, trying to avoid bringing Anna and Ginger into the conversation. Jackson paused with the sandwich halfway to his mouth and twisted towards her. Seeing her worry, he set his sandwich down on his plate and grabbed her hand. "I'm fine, Liz. Plus, you are paying for our work." He winked and made her laugh. Squeezing her hand he released it and went back to eating his sandwich.

«CHAPTER TWELVE»

Liz found herself a bit overwhelmed as she stood in Ginger Dean's kitchen. She felt somewhat traitorous, yet somewhat at ease. As her inward struggle continued, she could hear Ginger and Anna enjoying conversation. She looked up from dicing the plump green peppers and marveled at the beautiful kitchen in the Dean home. Unlike the Montgomery house, the Dean home held the appearance of a pre-Civil War home, but inside it boasted modern amenities and design. She ran a hand over the smooth countertop. The sun lit the surface as it shined through the large paned window. The kitchen was light and airy, Liz realized, with its exposed shelving, floor to ceiling windows, French doors open and leading to a stone laden patio, and herbs along every surface. *If she could have any kitchen,* she thought, *it would be one like this.* And though the kitchen held modern appliances and design decisions, it retained its original architecture with ornate ceilings and molding. Wooden floors that boasted scuffs, scratches, and well-worn paths gave the space part of its history. The myriad of mixing bowls, dishes, glasses, and utensils lining the exposed shelves lent stories all their own, as Liz wondered how they'd been used over the years. Liz loved it, and she hoped, once they finished the bones of the east wing, she could tell Jackson just what to do for her own kitchen.

"Earth to Liz," Anna snapped her fingers and Liz blinked away her thoughts as she found both women staring at her.

"I'm sorry, did I miss something?"

"We were just asking you for the peppers." Anna pointed at the mound of green pieces in front of Liz and Liz laid down her knife.

"Oh, I'm sorry. I was just admiring the kitchen." She smiled at Ginger. "It's beautiful."

"Why thanks, sugar. Jackson did it for me about three summers ago."

"Jackson did this?" She looked around with a whole new appreciation at his skill.

"Yes ma'am, he did."

"I didn't realize he'd lived here that long," Liz added, as she handed her peppers to Anna and watched as her friend separated them into three separate bowls.

"He hasn't," Ginger continued. "He used to just visit for long spells at a time when he could get away. And a few summers ago, I told him to bring that tool belt of his because I had a project for him." She grinned. "I think he thought I needed a picture hung or somethin', not an entire kitchen. But that sweet boy took right to it and created my dream."

"Yes," Liz agreed. "It's stunning. I love your countertops. What are they made of?"

"Soapstone," Ginger answered. "I wanted a natural stone, but something a bit more unique than granite and marble. And it is so easy to take care of. Why, if I scratch it or somethin', you can just sand it right out, oil it up, and it's like nothin' ever happened." She smiled. "And Jackson felt it blended well with the overall design of the kitchen. Somethin' about it bein' used over a century ago in old farmhouses. So we thought it a good fit. He has an eye for these things. That boy is gifted. And he spoils me rotten." She laughed affectionately as she stirred one of the mixing bowls.

"So why did Jackson not grow up here?" Anna asked curiously.

"Oh, well, I'll tell ya." Ginger waved the women to two barstools as she left her mixing and retrieved three glasses from a shelf and poured them each a glass of sweet tea. "I think we've earned a break." She pointed to the foil pans lined up on the counter next to the double ovens. "Once we get these final three ready, we'll put them all in at the same time, that way they'll stay warm about the same." Anna and Liz nodded, neither one debating the logic behind her decision. "So, Jackson," Ginger began, "he was such a sweet boy, still is, but his daddy and Ronald had an altercation years ago and David, that's Jackson's daddy, left Quinton and swore he'd never come back. We didn't see Jackson for the first time until he was eleven years old." She put a hand over her heart as her eyes misted. "He was so sweet, but his poor eyes just looked lost. Bless his heart."

"What happened?" Anna's eyes were wide as she leaned forward, eager to hear the rest.

"Well," Ginger continued, "David had fallen in love with a woman named Rachel. He swore up and down that she was the woman for him. We had never met her, but apparently David had met her at some party and she was visiting a cousin. David was about... nineteen at the time, I believe. He was so adamant that she was the girl for him. He told us he was going to marry her."

"So then what happened?" Anna asked, taking a sip of her tea.

"He did. He and Rachel eloped before we could even meet her. Ronald was so upset and hurt. He and David had words, especially when we found out Rachel was from up north and David planned on moving up there. Ronald had hopes David would take over here, with the farmin' and such. But David stood his ground in such a way that Ronald lost his head. Told him he was no son of his and that if he wished to be a Yankee, so be it. That he wasn't welcome here anymore. We haven't seen David since."

Liz reached over and squeezed her hand. "I know that must be hard."

Ginger accepted the napkin Anna offered and dabbed her eyes. "It's always hard as a momma to see your babies leave the nest. But when they leave under such circumstances, it's heartbreakin'. David and Ronald both were at fault with their stubborn pride. David's marriage only lasted a year, but within that marriage, Jackson was born. Rachel had custody until she passed. Jackson was seven when that happened. He then went to live with David and his new wife, Rose. Rose has been good to Jack. She's his mother. He has very few memories of Rachel."

"How sad." Anna dabbed her own eyes.

"Ronald has regretted his words ever since, and has even attempted to mend fences with David, but David won't hear of it. He's still stuck in his ways. We thought, by sending Jack to us when he was eleven, that things would slowly start mendin'. But we quickly found out it was only so

David and Rose could vacation during the summertime. So every summer after that, Jack would come to visit for a short time."

"I don't think I had ever seen him before until I walked into the hardware store," Liz said. "You would think a Montgomery would know when a new Dean was in town, no matter how old he was at the time."

"Jack never went to town much. He loved helpin' Ronald on the farm. He found everything so fascinating. Such joy and wonder." Ginger smiled. "When Jack called to tell us he wished to move to Quinton, we were just ecstatic." Beaming, Ginger walked back over to the mixing bowl and started stirring. "He's been livin' in the guesthouse since he arrived. I know he wishes to have some space of his own, but I think he feels obligated to look after Ronald and me. Course he and Ronald are almost inseparable." She chuckled. "Ronald loves that boy, and we are so thankful for him."

"I'm glad he came to Quinton." Liz added, causing the other two women to eye her. "I mean, for yours and Ronald's sake," she quickly amended. "Though I won't deny I enjoy having the use of his skill as a contractor."

Anna reached for one of the other mixing bowls and looked at Ginger. "Liz is still in denial."

Hooting with laughter, Ginger turned to dump her contents into a foil pan.

"Hey now, denial? About what?" Liz asked, as she hopped down from her stool and intercepted the empty bowl from Ginger. Walking over towards the sink, she dipped it into the sudsy farm sink and began to wash it.

"You know what," Anna pointed out. "You and Jackson got somethin' goin' on."

Baffled, Liz turned, her jaw dropped. "Anna Marie Richards, lying does not become you."

Laughing, Anna pointed at Liz. "If I'm lyin', why is your face so red?"

"My face is not red." Liz turned back to her task, her back to the ladies. "Jackson is my contractor, and yes, I would like to think we have become friends in the process, but to say there is something more is a flat out lie."

"Okay, let me reword it then." Anna circled her hand in the air as if trying to come up with the right words. "Maybe somethin' isn't going on yet, but I think you and Jackson *want* something to go on."

"I have no idea what you're talking about," Liz muttered, as she set the bowl on a hand towel to dry. She accepted another empty bowl from Ginger and began washing again. "Besides, a Montgomery does not end up with a Dean. History proves that. And even though my grandmother and I are fighting at the moment, I do not wish to kill her by announcing such a union."

"Oh, Sissy." Ginger shook her head. "What that woman needs is a good whippin' for the way she's been treatin' you. Now I know she and I have never gotten on, but it's just not right. What I wouldn't give to have a sweet child like you wishin' to live with me. But though Sissy has acted a fool the last few days, I know she will soon come around. Look at Ronald. The whole situation with David speaks to that. He regretted his actions immediately. It just took him years to own up to them."

"Let's just hope it doesn't take Grandmother years to see I only want what's best for her," Liz added.

Ginger looped an arm around Liz's shoulders and squeezed. "I don't think she will, honey. Once she sees her beautiful kitchen, she would rather die than go back on her word. You'll be back in that house by tomorrow afternoon." With a wink, she walked over to the ovens and began sliding the pans in and swiped her hands on her apron. "Thirty minutes and then the men will be fed."

∞

Jackson looked up the stairwell and flexed his fingers as he wondered exactly what he wished to say to Sissy Montgomery. The breakers had been thrown twice that day already, and the third time had his temper rising. Bill emerged at the entrance of the kitchen and studied his boss. “Remember boss, you win more flies with honey than vinegar.”

Jackson turned and saw Bill’s suppressed smile.

“Why are you smiling at me like that?” Jackson asked.

“Because this is one of those moments I’m thankful I’m not the boss.” Bill chuckled and shook his head as he pointed up the stairs. “Better get to it. That conversation won’t start without ya.”

Jackson started up the stairs, Bill’s watchful eyes disappearing as he cleared the first landing and turned up the next stairwell to the west wing. He had yet to be over on this side of the house since Liz gave him the grand tour. And as he surveyed his surroundings, he wished he could breathe life back into the old house. He reached the door to the west wing banquet hall, the area he knew Sissy used as her main living quarters and knocked. Muffled footsteps sounded on the other side and Mitzy opened the door. Her eyes widened and she shut the door with just a smidgen of space left between them. “Mr. Dean, you best not be up here. Mrs. Montgomery would have a fit if she sees you.”

“I need to have a word with her, Mitzy. Immediately.”

"Mr. Dean, she won't see you."

"Mitzy, who is it?" Sissy's voice rang out and Jackson nudged the door further open and stepped over the threshold. Sissy stood by the large window overlooking the front yard holding a china cup in her hand. Her steely grey eyes held his as she set the cup on a small stand beside her. "Well, Mr. Dean, what brings you to my quarters?"

"I need to have a word, Mrs. Montgomery." He tried to relax his stance, but his anger and frustration battled with his patience as he watched her slowly wave a hand towards Mitzy.

"Leave us, Mitzy."

"Yes ma'am, Mrs. Montgomery." Mitzy flashed a worried glance at Jackson before stepping out, no doubt with her ear plastered to the other side of the door to listen.

"I do not allow Deans on my property, and yet here you are workin' on my house." Sissy began. "I do not allow Deans inside my house, and yet, you have been workin' in my kitchen the last two days and nights. I do not allow Deans in my personal quarters, and yet, here you stand. I'm beginnin' to think, Mr. Dean, that you have no respect for my rules."

"I don't," he admitted, causing her brows to rise. "However, on all three accounts, I have been admitted by someone in the household, so I have not barged into your home uninvited."

"Lizbeth's judgment doesn't count, as it has been skewed."

"I think that is a patently false statement," Jackson challenged, "but I did not come up here to start an argument with you, Mrs. Montgomery. I came up here to tell you that your kitchen is finished, and that your deadline was met, despite your hopes of sabotage. Liz should be allowed to move back into the house."

"Sabotage? What on Earth are you accusin' me of, boy?"

He held up the disc player and pressed play, the sounds of weeping filled the room until he stopped the player. "This was found in the passage ways. I have had crewmen leave because they believe a ghost haunted the grounds. Breakers have been manually flipped so as to stop all work. The urn through the window... I had three crewmen leave the job because of that incident alone. You have tried every way in the world to stop our work, and yet, here I am, telling you it's completed."

"I have done no such things, and your accusations—"

Jackson held up his hand as he stepped forward, her conversation halting. "I don't need to hear your excuses, Mrs. Montgomery. I've just come to let you know that despite the acts of hostility towards my crew and me, we completed the job. And we did not do it for you. We did it for Liz."

Sissy straightened her shoulders. "I think you'd best leave, Mr. Dean."

"I'm not finished," he continued. "I would like to escort you downstairs to see your kitchen. Liz has not seen it yet and does not know it's completed. I thought I would give you first glimpse."

"Why?"

"Because I have a feeling your deadline was an attempt to punish Liz for not only allowing my working here, but to also prove a point."

"And what point would I be tryin' to prove to my granddaughter?"

"That your grief is more important than hers."

Sissy gasped, "Well, I never." Her cheeks flushed with anger as she stepped towards him, her cane thumping as she came.

"Mrs. Montgomery, I spent the majority of my life barely able to visit my grandparents. I also spent the majority of my life wondering why they could possibly turn my father away. It wasn't until I was older that I realized my grandfather exchanged hurtful words with my father. Words that neither man has ever forgotten. My father has not seen my grandfather since he was nineteen years old, ma'am. I didn't see my grandparents until I was eleven."

"That has nothing to do with me, please leave."

"It has everything to do with you, if you would just listen." Jackson stepped forward, his shoulders relaxing and his voice pleading in such a way, Sissy halted her protests and gave her full attention.

"Due to that hurt, I missed out on time with my grandparents. Time I wish I could take back tenfold. Now imagine, Liz. She was raised by you. You have been her mother, at least the only mother she's ever known. She loves you. Cherishes you, even. And she has broken her back trying to please you. So she screws up every now and then, we are human. It happens. But your words to her the other day will never be undone unless you choose to undo them. Pride is a scary foe, Mrs. Montgomery. I've personally experienced how it can tear a family apart. If you want to spend the rest of your life alone in this big, empty house, then don't honor your word. But, if you secretly wish those words had never been spoken in the first place, I ask that you come to see your new kitchen. The one Liz helped design for you, because she loves you." He waited a moment as he watched his words sink into the older woman's head. He could see her weighing her options, and she slowly began walking towards the door.

Opening it, she stepped out into the hallway. "I will need help down the stairs." Her statement gave a small boost to his step as he offered his arm to her and began leading her to the kitchen.

When they reached the downstairs, he pulled away the plastic curtain dividing the kitchen apart from the rest of the house and Sissy gasped. Her eyes landed on her dinette table. The table she had seen crushed now sat before her as if nothing had ever happened to it. Centered in the middle was a fresh bouquet of pink roses, their scent carrying across the room. Her eyes then went to the new cabinets, countertops, and appliances. The walls were painted a soft grey, and the outside light flooded the room and brightened the space and the mood. Her chandelier was hung above the table, just like it always had been, her coffee station was where she had placed it herself over twenty years ago, only it boasted a new surface upon which to rest. The pot rack hanging from the ceiling above the bar displayed her copper-bottom pots, all newly polished and gleaming in the sun's rays. It was beautiful, and she felt the crushing wave of self-disgust as she thought back on her words to Elizabeth. Shame filled her as she tried to muster enough words for a thank you, but instead, she accepted the napkin which Jackson handed her, not realizing her cheeks streamed with tears. "You may finish your work in the east wing, Mr. Dean." And without another word, Sissy walked away.

∞

Jackson sat at the small dinette table in the Montgomery kitchen awaiting Liz and Honey. His crew had long since gone home, and he felt the exhaustion of the last few days slowly sinking into his limbs. The heaviness of sleep threatened to overtake him, but he perked up at the sound of tires on gravel. Doors shut and he walked out onto the patio to meet a confused Liz as she held pans of food in her hands. "Where's the crew?" Her eyes held questions and worries as she tried to peer past him into the kitchen. "I sent them home. No more work can be done today."

"Oh." The simple syllable almost made him laugh as the dejected look on her face carried over towards his grandmother.

"We made casseroles." Honey announced. "What are we to do with these?"

Jackson shrugged. "Set them on the saw tables." The women did as he suggested and Liz perked up as Lucille bounded out the open patio doors and straight to her. "Hey girl, how have the men been treatin' ya?" She rubbed behind the dog's ears and then nudged Lucille's paws from her pant leg back to the ground. "Tell me what is going on, Jackson." Liz started to cross her arms, but Jackson reached out and took her hand, linking her arm through his. "Allow me, Ms. Montgomery, to show you your new kitchen."

Her eyes widened. "It's finished?" Her whisper of surprise had him nodding proudly.

"It is. Would you like to see it?"

She nodded as he escorted her through the doors into the newly renovated space. Tears flooded her eyes as she squealed in delight. Jumping, she threw her arms around his neck in a tight embrace. "Oh, Jackson it's beautiful!" She released him and stepped further into the room, running her hand over the smooth countertops. "Soapstone, nice choice." She sent a small wink at Ginger as she continued around the room. She ran her hand over every surface until her eyes landed on the dinette table. "Wait," she looked over at him. "How?"

"My grandfather has a way with wood. He helped me get this baby back together."

"Oh, Jackson, Grandmother is going to love that." She felt a tear slide down her cheek as she glanced at her watch. "And all of this was completed with one hour to spare. Looks like you met your deadline, Mr. Dean."

"Actually, the work was completed three hours ago." He corrected with a proud tilt to his chin. "I just did not want to ruin the surprise."

"I should go tell Grandmother, so that she sees it is complete. She'll be watching the minutes." Liz rubbed her hands over her cheeks but could not suppress the smile on her face.

"She's already seen it."

"What?" Liz asked. "When?"

"A couple of hours ago. I went and spoke with her."

"You spoke with her?" Liz asked in shock.

"I did. She came, saw, and has given permission for work to continue on the east wing," Jackson explained.

"I- I don't know what to say."

Jackson grinned as Ginger stepped forward and looped her arm around Liz's shoulders. "I say, we all fix a plate and have some casserole in this lovely new kitchen."

Biting back a laugh while she cried, Liz nodded. Anna stepped forward to retrieve plates, squeezing Jackson on the arm as she passed, a pleased twinkle in her eye. He pulled out a chair for Liz and then for Honey. Honey froze a moment. "Oh, dear. I didn't think of this. I should go. You three have a nice lunch. Jack, I will see you when you get home." Ginger squeezed his shoulder as she started to pass by, but Liz reached out to grip her arm. "Please, stay, Ginger. We would love it if you joined us."

Patting Liz's hand, Ginger shook her head. "I wouldn't want Sissy to see me here and get upset, sweetie. Let's leave things on a good note for today. Maybe some other time." Liz watched her leave and shook her head. "I think she should stay. Besides, she helped make all this food."

"Maybe another time." Jackson took a bite of the casserole and felt his stomach forgive him for the gallons of coffee he had consumed the last several days. "She wouldn't want to jeopardize your situation here, Liz."

"It's still ridiculous that we have to think of such things."

"Again," Anna added, "in time. Wounds heal with time."

∞

Sissy Montgomery stood outside the doorway to the kitchen and listened to the conversation around her table. Ginger Dean had actually respected her wishes and left. Ginger was a nice woman, Sissy admitted, but she couldn't help but still have lingering anger towards the woman, especially now that George was gone.

She thumped her cane on the floor as she stepped forward so that the crowd in the kitchen would sense her presence. Glancing up, Liz's smile held nerves. "What do you think of the kitchen, Grandmother?"

Sissy's eyes flashed over Jackson sitting at her table eating before landing back on Liz. "I find it quite nice." She headed towards the cabinet to retrieve a plate and helped herself to some casserole. "Mind if I join you three?"

"Not at all." Anna pulled out the last remaining chair and Sissy sat.

An awkward silence fell over the table. Jackson cleared his throat as he stacked his silverware on his plate. "Well, I should go. I feel like I could sleep all day and night now that I have a full stomach."

"You probably *should* sleep that long."

He smiled at Liz's statement. "I probably will so that I can be here bright and early tomorrow to start back on the east wing."

"Take a day off, Jackson," Liz said. "East wing can wait. Besides, I haven't even had a chance to speak to grandmother to see if I'm allowed back in the house."

"Of course you are," Sissy said without hesitation. She did not elaborate but continued eating her supper.

Bewildered, Liz looked up at Jackson and he winked. "I'll see you tomorrow, Liz." He held her gaze a moment longer before nodding a farewell to the other women and leaving. Liz followed him with her eyes as he made his way to his truck. She hated seeing him leave, but knew he was tired and needed rest. She had hoped they would have a moment alone to talk about the east wing. *Oh, who was she kidding? She just wanted a moment alone with him to talk to him about anything.* She found she looked forward to seeing him, to see him work, to see him with his crew. She liked seeing him, and she enjoyed talking with him. And after Ginger's glimpse into his past, Liz found him even more endearing.

∞

Sissy watched Liz as she stared after the Dean boy, and she knew her granddaughter had lost her heart to the boy. She wasn't quite sure how she felt about that, but she could see the looks of love washing over Liz's face. She wondered if Liz knew how she felt yet, or if she realized Jackson felt the same way about her. *Probably not,* Sissy mused. *Those in love never realize it unless it explodes right in their faces.* At least, that had been her experience with George. She was so hung up on Ronald Dean that she had overlooked George for years. What she wouldn't give for more time with George. Her heart ached with a renewed sense of loss and she felt tears burn the back of her eyes. She willed them away as Anna slapped a hand over Liz's arm to draw her attention back to the table.

"Ouch!" Liz rubbed her wound and glowered at her friend. "What was that for?"

"For drooling over Jackson."

"I was not drooling." Liz picked up her fork and took a bite of casserole.

"Oh really?" Anna opened her mouth and stared vacantly across the table.

Liz laughed. "That is not what I looked like."

"Um, pretty close. Right, Mrs. Montgomery?" Anna asked Sissy.

Sissy couldn't help the chuckle that slipped out. "You were staring, dear."

Liz's cheeks flushed. "Well, I was just making sure that he... well, he needed to... okay, I was staring." With reddened cheeks, Liz bent her head down and focused on her food.

"It is not polite to stare," Sissy scolded, though her tone held a sense of jest as she ate a bite of casserole.

Liz looked up and caught her Grandmother's apologetic stare.

"You are welcome to continue using the guestroom, Lizbeth, until Jackson has completed the east wing," Sissy announced.

"Thank you, Grandmother." Liz hoped for more, but Sissy remained quiet until she scooted her plate towards the center of the table and rose from her seat. "I also assure you there will be no more threats of ghosts haunting this house."

Baffled, Liz looked up at her. "Ghosts? What? Did you figure it out?"

"The problem has been taken care of." Sissy brushed her fingertips over her white hair before turning to leave the room. When she exited, Anna's eyes widened.

"What is that supposed to mean?" she asked.

"I have no idea," Liz said. "Guess she figured it out."

«CHAPTER THIRTEEN»

Jackson placed the trinkets in a box by the crawl space opening as he pulled himself out from under the house. Though he found no skeletons, he did find a few more fascinating objects on his quest under the Montgomery house. He stood, wiping his hands on his pant legs as he saw Liz's car pull into the drive. She carried several grocery bags and made her way towards the patio entrance. He waved her down and then bent to pick up his box. Carrying it towards her, he watched as her back stiffened slightly when he approached. "Hey, Liz," he greeted.

"Hey, yourself. What do you have there?"

"I found a few things under the house, thought you might like to see them."

"Sure. You can set them on the patio table and I will look at them when I get a moment."

Her quick dismissal surprised him. Confused, he slid the box onto the patio table and reached for one of her grocery bags. "Here, let me help you." She avoided his help by pulling away from him towards the house. "I've got it, thanks." She turned her back towards him and walked into the kitchen. He lingered by the door a moment. "Is everything okay?"

She looked up. "Of course."

"Are you sure?" he asked, still perplexed by the cold shoulder she seemed to cast his way. He stepped into the room and her head snapped up. Stepping from around the counter she walked towards him, all but nudging him back out the doors. "I appreciate you collecting the things from under the house, but today is not a good day to chat."

He held up his hands as if acquiescing to her insistent pushing. "Alright."

She heard the doubt and confusion in his voice and she regretted placing it there. "I'm sorry, Jackson. I have just been thinking. Other than house repair discussions, I think we should keep our conversations to a minimum. I just earned my right to live here again, and I don't really want to jeopardize that, you know?"

"I see."

She could tell her words did not make him happy as his eyes flashed and his jaw tightened. She didn't know what else to say, so instead of saying anything, she reached for the door to the patio and closed it, giving him no choice but to walk away. Anger heated each step he took as he headed towards his truck and slammed the door before studying the house through the windshield. *What had just happened?* Sissy had loved the kitchen. She had allowed Liz to move back in and for work to continue on the house. Sissy had even tolerated him around the house now. So why was Liz pulling back all of a sudden? Had Sissy forbade her to see him? Or to speak to him? *Nonsense.* Liz had just spoken to him, so that wasn't it. Irritated, he slammed a palm down on the steering wheel as he cranked the engine and nudged his truck into reverse. If Liz wished to keep their interactions professional, so be it. He could be professional. He was a professional. Though he couldn't ignore the disappointment lingering in his chest, he bit back the bitter taste of it and made his way towards the hardware store.

It did not help his mood any when he saw Ben's smiling face behind the counter. Ben's grin faltered when Jackson shoved the swinging door with more force than necessary as he headed towards his office.

"Bad day?" Ben asked.

"You could say that," Jackson growled as he sat in his desk chair and began punching keys at his computer. He decided an office day was in order. He would key in supply orders and go over the budget for the Montgomery property and completely forget about his encounter with Liz.

"So I received a text from Anna earlier," Ben said, Jackson not even glancing up from his screen.

"About Liz." He didn't hide his smug smirk as Jackson's head popped up immediately. "Thought that might get your attention."

Jackson bit back a snide remark and ground his teeth as he tried to wait patiently for Ben to keep talking.

Relaxing, Ben shoved his hands in his pockets.

"And?" Jackson asked.

"Seems Liz has been in quite a mood."

"I gathered that on my own, thanks."

"What happened out at the property?" Ben prodded.

Jackson slammed his hand down on the desk and tried to contain his exasperation. "She all but ignored my presence. The thought of even speaking to me disgusted her it seemed. She avoided me like the plague and all but slammed the door in my face. Fed me some lines about keeping our conversations to a minimum."

"Ah, yeah, Anna said something about that too. Liz is treading pretty cautiously around Sissy. Doesn't want to risk hurting her or disappointing her again."

"Ridiculous," Jackson muttered under his breath. "I thought we were past all this?"

Ben shrugged. "Can't blame her though. I mean, Sissy can be tough, sure, but she's the only family Liz has left. She just wants to make sure things run smoothly."

Shaking his head, Jackson focused back on his screen. The numbers and words kept running together as he couldn't focus past the anger boiling in his veins.

"I'll leave you to chomp on that for a bit." Ben turned to leave and paused. "Just give her some space for a few days. Liz will come around, she always does."

Grunting, with what Ben could not decipher as agreement or dismissal, Jackson ignored him as he walked back to the front counter.

∞

Two months passed by and little had been spoken between Jackson and Liz. Conversations about remodeling plans had been minimal at best, and Jackson found that those conversations were in too short supply. He typed up a daily report and left it for her in the kitchen at the end of each week. Liz scarcely showed her face anymore, and Sissy Montgomery made sure her presence was known at every corner. Mitzy had been scarce as well, as Jackson had found out she had been behind all the sabotage incidents. Not from Liz, but Ben had filled him in on that bit of news via Anna. He still grew upset thinking about the old maid tampering with his projects and scaring away his crew. Her misguided loyalty to Sissy and her wishes to leave the house untouched had convinced the maid to take matters into her own hands. Liz never spoke to him about it all.

He looked up as he heard Lucille's claws tapping on the patio stones as he sat pouring over the plans for Liz's wing of the house. They had completed her new kitchen, of which Liz had left detailed plans, wishes, and instructions through email. Now his work continued through the rest of the wing, turning it into a modern apartment-style home. He absentmindedly rubbed a hand over Lucille's head and patted her side as she leaned into his calf. He marked off a measurement sequence on the blueprint as he heard the patio doors open.

"Oh," Liz paused as if caught sneaking out of the house.

Jackson looked up and offered a smile. "Hey."

"Hey, I didn't realize you were out here working." As she stood in the doorway, teetering between continuing outside or retreating back into the house, all seven puppies stumbled over ears and feet to make their way outside. Jackson smiled as several rushed towards his shoes and began fighting over who deserved the privilege to chew upon his laces. He reached a hand down and met wet tongues and eager little bodies awaiting a pet. He caught the smile Liz tossed his way as she continued outside. "They've gotten big."

She nodded. "Yes, won't be long before they start venturing to their respective homes. Kind of sad to think about really."

"You already have them all a place?"

"All but a couple. Want one?" She grinned as she leaned her hands over the back of a patio chair.

"I'm tempted. Though I do not think you are willing to part with the one I want."

"Dean is spoken for." She tempered a soft laugh as the puppy raised his head at his name. "He's a smart one, and has kind of won my heart."

Jackson studied her a moment, until Liz looked up to find his gaze upon her. Clearing her throat, she stood. "I'll take them around front so they won't bother you."

"They're fine," He hurried to say, "Besides, I could really use some of your input on the plans."

She glanced at her watch and then nervously at the house. "I really can't right now, Jackson. I'm sorry. I'm on my way to town for Grandmother."

"It will only take a second, Liz." He saw the longing in her eyes, that brief flicker of regret as she shook her head. "Just leave me a note in the kitchen and I'll get back to you today." She began to usher the puppies towards the front of the house.

"This is ridiculous, Liz." Jackson stood, his chair teetering a moment as puppies retreated quickly after Liz. She paused at the edge of the house, her eyes burdened by more than just remorse. Shaking her head, she disappeared around the house. He caught a movement behind the glass of the French doors of the kitchen and saw Sissy watching him closely. He lowered back to his chair and steadied his breathing. *He would hold his tongue, for Liz's sake, but he didn't have to look happy about it.* He ignored Sissy's presence until he saw her move away from the doors. It was then he tapped his pencil on the plans in front of him. His desire to continue this project was waning with every passing day.

∞

"This place has come a long way." Anna stood proudly in the boutique, hands on her hips as she surveyed the latest paint job on the walls. The pale mint color felt warm and inviting as the dark-stained wood shelving lined the room. "It's going to look beautiful, Liz."

"Thanks."

"Has Jackson seen it?"

"No. Not for a while."

"You should tell him to come take a look. He'd be impressed with all your work."

Liz shrugged. "He's busy."

Anna watched her friend as she shifted an empty clothing rack into position, the bronze fixture angled between two shelving units.

"I don't think he is too busy to come see you."

"Anna," Liz warned as she walked towards another fixture and began moving it.

"Don't *Anna*, me." Anna shook her finger at Liz. "You have been giving him the slip the last two months. What's up with that?"

"You know what's up," Liz continued, brushing past her into the back room to retrieve several boxes of merchandise and placing them on the newly crafted cash wrap.

"You give your grandmother way too much control over your life, Liz."

Huffing, Liz turned to Anna, her eyes clouded by unshed tears. "I don't want to talk about this. Now can you please help me hang these clothes on the back wall?"

"I think we *need* to talk about this. You obviously still have feelings for Jackson. And he definitely has feelings for you. Ben said he's been crotchety and miserable since you started shunning him."

"I have not shunned him. I simply started treating our relationship like a professional one, which it is."

"Yeah right," Anna retorted. "Keep telling yourself that. But your dismissal of him as a friend has been pretty ugly."

Liz turned back to her boxes, trying to ignore the fact that Anna's words were true. She knew her actions towards Jackson had been rude and dismissive, but she couldn't think of any other way to drive the point home to him that nothing could happen between the two of them. Her grandmother, though past the kitchen incident, still held him in low regard due to him being a

Dean. And Liz knew nothing would ever change her mind. Her relationship with her grandmother had blossomed the last few weeks, and she credited it to her own decision of not allowing a Dean to come between them. No matter how she felt about Jackson, or wanted to feel about him, she couldn't mess up the relationship between her and her grandmother.

She heard the door open and glanced up to find Ginger Dean walking in, her oversized purse hanging in the crook of her arm and her high heels clicking on the newly polished floor. She lowered her sunglasses and surveyed the room. "Well, Elizabeth, I must say this is a beautiful store. I cannot wait to see what you fill it up with. Oh, are those scarves?" She patted the silk scarf that covered her hair and walked towards the shelf containing the new merchandise. "Lovely, just lovely." She then turned her attention to the two women. Anna smiled in greeting, and Liz looked miserable just like Jackson. She shook her head and tisked her tongue as she walked towards Liz and enveloped her in a tight hug. "Sweetheart, you look about as dour as Elizabeth Bennett after learnin' her sister ran off with Mr. Wickham."

"Doesn't she?" Anna agreed, waving her hand as if Ginger's statement was proof of her previous conversation.

Liz pulled away from the hug and forced a polite smile. “No gloomy faces here. I’m perfectly fine. What brings you by, Mrs. Dean?”

“Mrs. Dean, is it? I thought we had agreed you would call me Honey or Ginger?” She waved a hand. “Never mind that right now though. I came by because I wanted to ask you why you have rejected my grandson as of late.”

“Rejected?” Liz shook her head and continued lining the shelves with product. “I have not rejected Jackson. We work fine together.”

“Work fine together?” Ginger’s distaste in the comment rang in her drawn out tone of disappointment. She looked at Anna baffled. “My, my, my… you were right to call me.”

Liz’s head popped up to look at Anna and her friend grabbed her purse. “I’ll be back in a few. I’m going to run to see Ben for a few minutes, let you two talk.” Without another word, Anna disappeared out the door leaving Liz with Ginger.

Liz placed her hands on her hips. “I do not understand why everyone thinks something is wrong between Jackson and me. We are fine. He’s my contractor. Always has been. He’s remodeling my house and doing a fine job.”

“Sweetheart, please, let’s sit.” Ginger motioned to two stools and took residence on the first one, setting her purse on the counter. Liz walked over and sat.

"Jack has worked so hard on your house. He's poured his heart into it. He loves what he does, that is for sure, but that house has become so special to him. Or at least, I thought it was the house. But the more he spoke about the place and the project, it wasn't that house that had won him over. It was you, Elizabeth. Jackson loves you. Now I know it may seem a bit hasty, but that boy has not shut up about you from the moment he met you."

Liz crossed her arms as she listened, crossing her legs as well. She could not believe Jackson would send his own grandmother to try and talk to her about his feelings. Then again, Ginger tended to poke her nose in everyone's business despite their wishes, so perhaps he didn't know. "Listen, Ginger, I appreciate you coming here and sharing… this… all with me," Liz began, "but Jackson and I barely know one another. Were we friends, yes, I would like to think so, but I have to do what's right for me. And being friends with him, unfortunately, is not. I know your family has moved past the Montgomery/Dean feud, but my grandmother has not. And as long as I live in Montgomery House, I will abide by her wishes. I'm sorry, but I cannot be friends, or anything other than a professional acquaintance, with Jackson."

"Hogwash!" Ginger stood up, her hands flying in the air as she reached for her purse. "Anna said you were brainwashed, now I am startin' to believe it. Sweetie, you have got to start livin' for you. Sissy may not like my Jack, but you do, and you know him better than she does. I think, as a grown woman, you can determine your friendships."

"I understand your feelings, Mrs. Dean."

The formality irritated Ginger, but all it did was fuel her further. "You take care, Elizabeth." She slid her sunglasses on her face. "I'll be seein' ya real soon."

Abruptly, the matriarch of the Dean family sashayed outside and down the street, her sudden departure curious.

Liz shook her head as she returned to unloading boxes. "Love," she muttered on a hiss, "we barely know each other." She placed several more scarves on the shelf, her eyes growing misty as she kicked the empty box on the floor. *This was stupid.* But as stupid as she felt for ignoring Jackson the last couple of months, she felt even more ridiculous when she realized that she loved him anyway. Despite the fact he'd never vocalized his feelings, she felt his heart towards her too. Or *did*, before she had turned him away. There was something special between them starting to stir before she decided to appease her grandmother. But as much as she longed to test Ginger's words, she did not want to risk her relationship with her grandmother. Things were finally reaching a new normal for them. Despite the harsh treatment in the beginning, Sissy had warmed considerably over the last several weeks, and Liz did not wish to destroy what progress had been made. However, the thought of seeing Jackson had her moving listlessly through the boutique, shutting off lights and locking doors, and hurrying to her car.

«CHAPTER FOURTEEN»

Jackson cringed as he saw his grandmother's car pull into the circle drive of the Montgomery House. He was wrapping up for the day and could not, for the life of him, think of a good reason why his grandmother needed to speak to him now and not at home in fifteen minutes.

She waved as she approached, her gait unsteady as her heels sunk in the surrounding grass on her way towards him. "Honey, what brings you here?"

"Hi, Sweetheart." She kissed his cheek and continued onward towards the patio doors.

He hurried after her as she reached for the door knob. "Whoa, whoa, whoa, what do you think you're doing?"

Ginger looked up at him. "Why, I'm goin' to have a little conversation with Sissy, Jack. Now if you will excuse me."

"What? No, you cannot go inside the house. Honey, Sissy Montgomery will not want to see you. Are you trying to get me fired?"

Ginger placed a hand over his arm. "Jackson, please release the door knob."

He hesitated a moment before he caught her stern glare. His hand slowly slid from the knob and into his pocket. "Why do you need to speak to Sissy?"

"That is my business. Now if I'm not home in an hour, send the police, because she's likely killed me." Ginger, a bit of teasing in her voice, but edged with a touch of concern, walked into her rival's home.

She found her way to the stairwell as Mitzy was walking down, the maid's eyes widened in surprise. "Mrs. Dean? May I help you?"

"Yes, I am in search of Sissy, is she upstairs?" Ginger continued walking up the stairs. Mitzy, flabbergasted, hurried towards her. "I will escort you to the parlor and let Mrs. Montgomery know you're here."

"No need. I can meet her in her wing of the house. It's the west side, correct?" Ginger pointed as she continued up the steps and Mitzy hurried after her. "Ma'am, I, uh, well, I will need to see if she is up for company."

"You do that." Ginger paused outside the door of the west wing and waited as Mitzy slipped inside, shutting the door behind her.

∞

Jackson drummed his fingers on the patio table as he listened to the phone incessantly ring on the other end. "Come on, Liz," he muttered, "pick up."

"Hey, I was just about to call you." Her voice held irritation, and he tried not to sound disappointed.

"Oh?"

"It's about your grandmother."

"Funny, I was just about to call you about the same thing."

"What do you mean?" Liz asked, the edge to her voice slightly wavering.

"Well," she heard him sigh. "She just pulled up and barged into your house."

"*What*?" Liz panicked over the phone. "I'm on my way. You just let her walk in? Are you crazy?"

"I-Well-You see…" he trailed off, not really knowing how to respond. "Look," *it was his turn to be irritated*, he thought. "I have no idea why she is here, okay. It's not like I asked her to come by. Besides, short of restraining her by force, what was I supposed to do?"

He heard a groan on the other side of the line. "This could be bad, really bad."

Hearing the nerves in Liz's voice, he softened his tone. "Look, do you want me to go up there and see what's going on?"

"Are you kidding?" Liz barked. "No. That would only make matters worse."

"Fine." Kindness gone, he gripped his phone wishing he could throw it at something. "I'll meet you on the front porch."

"Fine." Liz hung up and it was less than five minutes when he heard her car rushing up the driveway.

∞

Mitzy had barely opened the door again when Ginger barged right past her into the room. "Blow it out your rear end, Sissy Montgomery!" she yelled as she stomped and clacked her way into the room to a shocked Sissy as she sat on her sofa.

"Excuse me?" Sissy slowly stood, her eyes narrowing. "I did not invite you inside. What are you doing inside my home?"

"I'm here to talk sense into you, that's what I'm doin'." Ginger sat in the chair across from Sissy and waited for Sissy to sit again. "By now, I imagine Jackson has alerted Elizabeth to my presence here, so we best start talkin' because my visit may be cut short."

Sissy waved her hand for Ginger to continue. "Since I am at a loss as to why you dare show your face on my property, I will allow you to speak first."

"Good." Ginger set her purse down and crossed her ankles as she began. "I do not think I have to explain to you how wonderful our two grandchildren are, and in case you are confused, I would like to clarify that I mean Jackson and Elizabeth. Jackson, meanin' my grandson, is a good man. And he has worked extremely hard on your home and he has worked to be as respectful as possible, though you have not treated him with equal respect."

"How dare you say such a th—"

Ginger held up her hand. "I am not finished. When I heard you whopped my grandson with that cane of yours, you better believe Ronald had to talk me down from comin' over here and doin' the same to you." She paused a moment and felt a sudden spurt of satisfaction when she saw the guilty flush wash over Sissy's cheeks. "Now I will chalk that up to a misunderstandin' and move on, but what I don't understand is this Montgomery versus Dean nonsense. Why are we still at war, Sissy? And why are you takin' it out on our grandkids?"

Sissy regained her composure and tilted her chin up as she studied Ginger. "You dare ask me that? After what you did?"

"What I did? If you are talkin' about Ronald, that was both our doin'. We loved each other, and George loved you. Why the fuss now? I know you hate me for ruinin' your chance at Ronald, but when you and George married, I'd never seen two people so happy. What has changed? And why must you stir such hatred in the heart of your granddaughter?"

"Lizzy hates no one. The girl is incapable of such a feeling," Sissy stated in defense. "As for me, I could not care less about you. My dislike comes from the way you flounce around town. The fact you are a Dean just reinforces my distaste."

"Absurd." Ginger waved her comments away and Sissy felt her skin heat with anger.

"I loved George," Sissy stated. "And there wasn't a day that went by that I wasn't grateful I did not marry Ronald Dean."

Confused and intrigued, Ginger crossed her hands in her lap as she heard car doors slam outside. Jackson had called Elizabeth after all, and she felt a small pleasure in that fact.

"I loved Ronald once, but it paled in comparison to my love for George."

"Then why the hate?" Ginger asked. "You have despised us for years."

"I disliked the underhandedness in which it all happened, yes, and I did not want my granddaughter to be swept away in the same way I was, and just be tossed aside as soon as a new pretty face arrived into town."

"Jackson would never do that to Elizabeth. That boy has been smitten with her from the moment he laid eyes on her," Ginger defended and noted the lack of surprise in Sissy. "But you knew that, didn't you?" she finished and waited for Sissy to continue.

"I will admit I began to pick up on the feelings between the two," Sissy continued, "that's when I knew I had to put a stop to them. Lizzy cannot be hurt, especially by a Dean. I want her to find her George. And every time I look at that boy down there, all I see is Ronald Dean. He is no George."

"Have you ever thought that Jackson is nothing like his grandfather?"

"He looks just like him," Sissy said, her voice holding a hint of regret. "Just like Ronald did at that age."

"He does." Ginger smiled tenderly. "And though Ronald and Jackson have a great relationship, Jackson is his own person. I find it unfair you judge his actions and his heart based on Ronald's. That is an injustice, Sissy, and you know it is."

Sissy said nothing.

"And Jackson could very well be Elizabeth's George. Who are we to stop them from seein' if that's true? My goodness, Jack has been slumpin' around like he lost his favorite puppy or somethin'. I've never seen him so down since Elizabeth stopped talkin' with him."

Sissy shook her head. "It's best this way, Ginger, and you know it is. Deans and Montgomerys don't mix."

"They could if stubbornness would allow them to," Ginger challenged.

"Stubborn?" Appalled, Sissy stood and walked over to the main window that overlooked the front yard. She saw Liz and Jackson conversing by the car, their gazes flashing towards the house every now and then. She could tell by Liz's stance and waving arms that she was giving Jackson a piece of her mind, and the thought pleased Sissy. Just as she saw the tenderness in which Jackson handled Liz's outburst. That too, pleased her.

"I'm sorry about George," Ginger stated, knowing full well what had captured Sissy's attention. "He was a decent man with a kind heart."

"He was," Sissy replied softly, her heart feeling the familiar squeeze at the thought of losing him. She watched as Jackson attempted to calm Liz and her granddaughter shoved him away, the hurt displayed on Jackson's face touched her heart. "You know, when George first passed, it seemed unreal."

Ginger stood and walked closer towards the window as Sissy began talking. They both watched their grandchildren argue down below.

"Then I saw you in town with Ronald, happy, enjoying one another. I felt so bitter. Why couldn't George still be here? I allowed the Dean and Montgomery feud to fuel my thinking so as to cover what I truly felt." Sissy resituated at the window so she could face Ginger. "Lost... and a bit jealous."

Ginger gripped Sissy's fingers, the mix of bright red nails with Sissy's pale pink showcased their different personalities as the two women teared up. "When Lizbeth first introduced me to Jackson, I sensed he was a Dean, but I did not know for sure. I couldn't place him in the lineup of your kids. I had forgotten about David, and I didn't realize he even had a son. But when I found out that boy was a Dean... it was just too much to take in all at once. I had just lost George and my sworn enemy was flouncin' her marriage right in front of me. She still had her husband. It just felt... unfair. Though I know it isn't your fault, or Ronald's for that matter. I just could not fathom having another Dean around me during my time of grief. And when I noticed Lizbeth's feelings towards the boy," she scoffed, "well, I could not have that. So yes, I tried to dissuade her, guilt her, and even punish her for interacting with the boy."

"And now?" Ginger pointed to the two out the window. "What now, Sissy?"

∞

"I cannot believe this." Liz finally pushed past Jackson and walked up the steps to the front door.

"Liz, wait, we should let them talk." Jackson hurried after her as she walked inside and charged up the stairs. "We haven't heard any gun shots yet, so I'd say it might be going pretty well."

Liz stopped a few steps ahead of him and turned around, her surprise at his statement had her briefly laughing. He grinned and she bit back her smile as she turned to hurry back up the remaining steps. She reached the top landing and startled an eavesdropping Mitzy.

"They in there?" Liz asked.

Mitzy nodded. "I wouldn't disturb them, Ms. Lizbeth."

Liz walked right past the maid and opened the door, Jackson hot on her heels.

Sissy and Ginger turned from the window, still hand in hand. Liz abruptly stopped, mouth agape, as she saw the two women smile at each other and then at her and Jackson.

"Grandmother, what is going on?" Liz asked, her voice slightly breathless from the climb up the stairs.

Jackson stepped forward and lightly placed his hand at the small of her back, a comforting gesture as she looked up at him as his face held equal confusion.

Sissy released Ginger's hand and walked towards Liz and cupped her face. "Lizzy, I need to apologize to you."

Liz's eyes flashed towards Ginger and then back towards her grandmother. "W-what?"

A tear slipped down Sissy's cheek as she pulled Liz into a tight hug. "I am so sorry, sweetie. So very sorry."

As her grandmother wept, Liz slowly raised her arms and encircled them around Sissy. Unsure what to say, she rubbed her grandmother's back until Sissy pulled back enough to cup her face again. "I have let my prejudice consume not only my life, but also yours. I have mistakenly kept you from... good friends." She looked to Jackson and reached for his hand as she eyed them both. "Forgive me."

"Grandmother," Liz's voice cracked as she hugged her grandmother once again. "I love you, of course I will forgive you. Shh, now. Calm down. Let me have Mitzy fix you some tea."

"No, no, no," Sissy waved away her concern. "Ginger and I are going to go to the café."

"Together?" Jackson asked curiously.

"Together." Ginger stepped forward and hugged him. "We have much to catch up on, as I assume you two do as well." She pinched his cheek before hugging Liz. "You be sweet to each other. Come Sissy, I think it's time for some refreshment." The two women walked out arm in arm. Liz looked up at Jackson and the confused expression they both held had her laughing. "What just happened?"

He ran a hand through his hair and blew out a long breath. "I have no idea. Did we miss something?"

Both turned towards Mitzy and the maid quickly exited the room before being cornered.

∞

"Can we talk now?"

"Well, I'm guessing so," Liz waved her hands to the retreating figures of their grandmothers.

"Good. Because not only would I like to be your friend again, but we need to talk remodeling plans."

"I never stopped being your friend, Jackson. I just—"

"Was trying to please Sissy," he finished for her. "I understand Liz… though I will admit that it made me extremely mad."

"I know, and I'm sorry for that. I was torn. I wasn't sure what to do anymore." She walked towards the stairs and headed down towards the patio, Jackson following suit. "It was easier to obey Grandmother and keep the peace. Though I will admit I missed talking with you." She nudged him with her shoulder.

"Me too." He winked at her as they sat at the table and he rolled out blueprints. She reached over and lightly touched the back of his hand causing his dark gaze to look up.

"I truly am sorry." Patting his hand she pulled hers back to her lap and then took a deep breath. "So, fill me in."

Jackson studied her a second longer before turning his attention back to the plans. As he explained the following week's schedule, Liz listened half-heartedly. Her gaze kept studying Jackson as he spoke.

Sensing her eyes on him, he looked up. "Something wrong?"

Blinking to clear her head, she smiled. "No, no please continue. Sorry, I just spaced out a minute."

"Alright, well, once we knock down that door and take out a portion of those walls, which will open up the space a bit, give the room more breathing room— Okay, what is it?" He turned to her again and found her looking at him instead of the plans before them.

Blushing, she focused upon the plans. "Nothing. I'm listening."

Pleased that he had caught her staring at him, he bit back a grin as he leaned back in his chair and crossed his arms. "You know what? I think we should forget plans right now and just hang out. We haven't gotten to in the last couple months."

"True, though I'm not sure if we should. I mean, our grandmothers are fine now, but maybe we should see how their lunch goes first."

He laughed. "Seriously?"

Liz's face held zero signs of kidding and he tried to sober as he leaned forward and grabbed her hand. "You know, I'm not sure when it happened, but I started wanting to spend more time with you. And not as your contractor."

She tried to hide the smile that threatened to burst through, but it slipped out and he blushed as he turned away for a moment to hide his reddened cheeks.

"Is that so?" she asked, causing him to turn back towards her.

He cleared his throat and nodded. "I know, completely unprofessional, and I completely understand if you do not feel the same way. I just—" his words were cut off as Liz planted a soft kiss to his lips. It was a light, teasing gesture that melted him even further. She smiled shyly as her cheeks flushed and she placed a palm to her face. "I cannot believe I just did that." Embarrassed, she shifted to rise, but he gripped her arm and pulled her back down to her chair. Moving his hand to her cheek he pulled her towards him and kissed her in return, a long, toe-curling kiss that had her heart thumping faster. When he pulled away, he lightly tucked her hair behind her ear. "Maybe now that our families seem to be moving on we can try to get to know one another on a friendlier basis?"

Liz shook her head and watched as disappointment fluttered over his handsome face, and though she wanted to tease him further, she couldn't help the laugh that escaped her lips. As soon as it did, he grabbed her around the shoulders and pretended to rub his knuckles over her head.

Squealing, she ducked out of his hold and smiled, her heart light as he leaned over and kissed her cheek. Rising, he reached out for her hand and Liz happily took hold. "Call me crazy, Mr. Dean, but I think I've taken a liking to you."

"Why, Ms. Montgomery, that's the best news I've had all day." He pointed to the box of trinkets on the table. "Perhaps you'll like me even more when you see what treasures I have discovered."

Liz's eyes lit with expectation.

"Particularly this one." He fished in the box and found an antique locket, the small hinge loose and the heart-shaped pendant swinging open to reveal two pictures.

"Who are they, I wonder?" Liz fingered the locket delicately as she held it in the palm of her hand.

"Oh, Jackson, this is so incredible." She held the locket to her heart and grinned.

Jackson's smile warmed her insides as he walked her towards his truck and opened the passenger door.

«EPILOGUE»

Liz stoked the fire with a poker as she heard the door to the east wing open and the now familiar sound of Jackson's keys being tossed onto the table by the door. She turned towards him and her smile grew as she saw the pizza box he held in his hands. "My hero."

He laughed as he walked towards the kitchen counter. "It is freezing out there, so we may need to pop this in the oven for a few minutes to warm up again." He pressed a few buttons and then slid the pizza onto a pan before sliding it into the oven. He then turned to Liz and enveloped her in a warm embrace. "How was your day, Mrs. Dean?" He lightly kissed her lips and Liz laid her head against his chest. "It was nice. Grandmother is ready for you to be done on her wing of the house. She called me twice today while I was at work to see what had you distracted today."

"Distracted?" He pulled back in surprise. "I was out buying her the new appliances she insisted upon."

Liz chuckled as she squeezed him tighter. "I know. I reminded her of that."

Shaking his head, he reluctantly released Liz. "I'm going to grab a hot shower before the pizza's ready." He kissed her forehead. "Have I told you how much I love you lately?"

Grinning, Liz nudged him towards the bathroom down the hall. "Only every second of every day."

"Ah, I guess I don't need to then." Winking, he disappeared around the corner calling out an 'I love you' as he went. She sighed, content and happier than she could ever imagine. Her gaze washed over her home, the east wing of the Montgomery House. Jackson's hard work and skill amazed her still. Her eyes landed on her wedding photo taken just a few short months ago. It was hard to believe she and Jackson were finally married. After her grandmother and Ginger had come to terms about the family rivalry, Jackson had asked Liz on a date that very day. Her heart warmed at the memory and she looked up as Lucille and Dean's nails clacked against the hardwood floors as they entered the kitchen. Dean, though only a year old, had surpassed his mother in size, but the young pup still remained a tender soul. She rubbed them both generously as she heard Jackson making his way back towards the kitchen. "Is it ready?"

She flinched. "I'm sorry, I haven't even checked on it."

He grabbed a dish towel and opened the oven, the pizza, just crisp around the edges. "Not too bad." He pulled it out and placed it on the stove top. Liz walked up behind him and slid her arms around him, resting her head in the middle of his back. "What has you so distracted?" he asked as he turned to face her, his arms still around her as he tilted her chin up towards him. He kissed her lightly on the lips.

"Everything," she answered. "I was just taking a moment to appreciate and admire our home and our life together. Every time I look at that picture," she pointed to their wedding photo, "I still feel the same joy I felt that day. Grandmother walking me down the aisle to you. The flowers from the garden arranged along the arch. Anna and Ben standing and waiting at the front. You in your tuxedo."

"Yeah, that won't ever happen again. Glad you caught it on camera."

She lightly poked his side as he grinned. "Your grandparents, sitting on the front row, on Montgomery property. And your dad coming."

"And all with smiles on their faces to boot." He turned in her arms and lightly tucked her hair behind her ear and fingered the antique locket around her neck. The locket he had discovered on his expedition under the house that contained a picture of two of Liz's ancestors.

"Smiles all around from what I remember. No more Montgomery/Dean feud, thanks to us. I'm thankful Grandmother shed her anger towards the Dean family." She squeezed him tighter for a moment and then released him as she walked to retrieve two plates.

"Me too. Otherwise, I would have had to kidnap you, elope with you, and convince you to live on Dean property."

"The scandal!" Liz feigned a gasp as Jackson laughed.

"It's a good thing Sissy came around. And that I wouldn't let you get rid of me." Jackson winked as she handed him a plate of pizza.

"You are a persistent one, Mr. Dean."

"Of which I am proud, now that I have you." He took a hearty bite of his slice as they walked towards the table and sat, Liz pouring them each a glass of red wine.

She reached for his hand. "I'm thankful for you, Jackson."

"And I you. Plus, I believe you are the prettiest Dean I've ever seen." He clinked his glass with hers and took a sip. "How could I have ever said 'no'"?

Choking on her sip of wine, Liz stifled a laugh as she coughed and lightly patted her chest. Rolling her eyes she shook her head as she took a bite of her supper and enjoyed the quiet comforts of Jackson and home.

All titles by Katharine E. Hamilton
Available on Amazon and Amazon Kindle

Adult Fiction:
The Unfading Lands
https://www.amazon.com/dp/B00VKWKPES

Darkness Divided, Part Two in
The Unfading Lands Series
https://www.amazon.com/dp/B015QFTAXG

Redemption Rising, Part Three in
The Unfading Lands Series
https://www.amazon.com/dp/B01G5NYSEO

Chicago's Best
The Lighthearted Collection
https://www.amazon.com/dp/B06XH7Y3MF

Children's Literature:
The Adventurous Life of Laura Bell
Susie At Your Service
Sissy and Kat

Short Stories:
If the Shoe Fits

Find out more about Katharine and her works at:

www.katharinehamilton.com

Social Media is a great way to connect with Katharine. Check her out on the following:

Facebook: Katharine E. Hamilton
https://www.facebook.com/Katharine-E-Hamilton-282475125097433/

Twitter: @AuthorKatharine
Instagram: @AuthorKatharine

Contact Katharine:
khamiltonauthor@gmail.com

ABOUT THE AUTHOR

Katharine E. Hamilton started her writing career a decade ago by creating fun-filled stories that have taken children on imaginative adventures all around the world. Katharine now extends the invitation to adults everywhere. She finds herself drawn time and again by the people behind her adventures and wishes to bring them to life in her stories.

She was born and raised in the state of Texas, where she currently resides on a ranch in the heart of brush country with her husband, Brad, and their son, Everett, and their two furry friends, Tulip and Cash. She is a graduate of Texas A&M University, where she received a Bachelor's degree in History. She finds most of her stories share the love of the past combined with a twist of imagination.
She is thankful to her readers for allowing her the privilege to turn her dreams into a new adventure for us all.